COMPRESSION

TIM CUNDLE

EARTH
ISLAND
BOOKS

Published by Earth Island Publishing
22 Church Road
Tunbridge Wells
Kent TN1 1JP
wwww.earthisland.co.uk
© Copyright Earth Island Publishing Ltd

First published by Earth Island Publishing 2019

ISBN 978-1-9997581-3-4

Printed and bound in Great Britain by Solopress

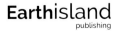

For Emma and Siobhan. Always.

With thanks

Thank-you: Ma for always being there no matter what.
Donna, Harriet and Jonathon, Molly Cook, Rhodri "Poggles" Dawe, Ian
Pickens, Jonathan "Satan" Evans and Matt "Porchie" Porch (the Cider Road
Trip brigade), Jim Dodge, Martijn Welzen, Chris Andrews, Tom Chapman,
Nathan Bean, Sophie Francois, Tony Fyler, Jason Thomas, Daniel Forst and
Mike Wild (the Mass Movement crew), my fellow Lantern Timothy
Schwader, Alan Wright – you're the best of us brother, Ian Glasper, Mark
"Splodge" Lodge (my partner in cinematic adventure), James "Jay X"
Connors for being the heart and soul of the Massive and so much more, All
Time Old Time (Gavin, Darrel and Chris) for riding 'Space Mountain' with
me, Charlies Family Crisis (Darren, Ian, Pixie, Tony and Sion) for four years
of blood, sweat, shows, demos and tears, Rachel Evans, Stephen Nanda,
Jethro Wall, Heath Crosby, Adam Caradog Thomas, Pete Williams, Michael
'Anyone for conkers?' Davies, Simon Phillips and Cheap Sweaty Fun for
twenty years of punk rock mayhem, George Tabb, Mike Beer City, Brady
Webb, Joel Meadows and Tripwire, Dean Jeffrey Beddis, Wayne 'Pig' Cole,
Welly and Artcore, Doug W. Marohn, Kathryn Coleman, Chris Kyle, Anna
Hinds (you'll always be Kuhlmann to me), Ross O'Brien for being a
belligerent old Goth, Alexandros "Alex" Anesiadis, Richard "Don
Doomcock" Torres, David "Dog" O'Grady, Paula Harris, David Gamage,
Marcus "Mivvi" Davis, Beth Dewhurst, Tim "Bunky" Davies, John Joseph
because PMA isn't just about three letters, Pat Mills, Neil Randle & Bang-
On, Blaine & The Accused AD, Mousetalgia for keeping the spirit alive, Paul
Bearer & Sheer Terror, Bad Religion, Youth of Today, D.O.A., Slapshot,
Crumbsuckers Underdog, Agnostic Front, Ratos De Parao, The Bruisers,
Circle Jerks, Pennywise and all the other bands whose music kept me going
when all else failed, Marvel Comics, DC Comics, Dark Horse Comics,
2000AD, Cardiff Devils, Flipside, WWE, ROH, ISW, ICW and FWA. And to
everyone else who has ever offered a kind word and a pat on the back, it was
appreciated more than you'll ever know.

Dedicated to the memory of Leslie Donald Cundle.
Until the next life you crazy old bugger. Slainte.

"There's a shadow on the wall where the paint is peeling
My body's moving forward but my mind is reeling
Depression is a fundamental state of mind
It doesn't really matter how my day has turned out I always end up
living in this world of doubt…"

'Sanity' – Bad Religion

Lyrics by Brett Gurewitz, © Universal Music Publishing Group

Foreword

Compression is a short sharp shock – a punk rock novel that's not directly about punk rock. Written in the tough and linear prose of the form, it offers a compelling and sulphate speckled rush through the grotty underbelly of the real UK.

Broken hearts and broken bodies fill a semi-autobiographical romp through the claustrophobic undergrowth of the UK told with a dense thicket of words.

If all the best British culture comes from the claustrophobia of our crowded island and its dark soul, then Compression captures this suffocation. The book tells it like it is without ever losing focus and with a love of 'words'.

Tim Cundle loves words.

He writes for a living in music where no one gets paid anymore. He writes about the forgotten and the fucked up and he knows their voices. The ongoing narrative in the book is observed perfectly. The voices are caustic, real and confused.

Words are all we have now after the bastards have robbed us of everything else. Language is the last flower that they cannot crush. The last raging torrent of freedom. That's why we treasure these wordsmiths. These poets of the dark metallic dawn; these poets of the brooding apocalypse; and these poets still fired by the aesthetic of the punk wars that shaped and moulded and ultimately made our lives impassioned and difficult and yet in full colour.

Anyone who grew up in that mess of contradictions will recognise this energy that rushes through the book. They will embrace the grubby minutia of a life full of waking up feeling like the worst hangover that Dean Martin ever had. This is a world full of hungover carpeted mouths, broken hearts, random stupid violence and wild eyes remoulded by the cruelty of chemical excess.

The book is like life. It's full of impatient narrative. It's hungry with the grinding shit talk and snark of modern rainy day UK – that lacerating humour and that embrace of the cracked concrete cancer of the council estates and broken junctions that seem to go nowhere.

Somewhere in the middle of all this is a great story – a romantic tale of human nature surrounded by the post-industrial clank and grind and the pre-digital humdrum of the last days of our cities in the late 20th century before they slipped from post-industrial wasteland to post punk smooth lines without ever losing the hangover stench of grey skies and cruel dreams.

Like a classic two minute single from that machine gun of musical dreams in the late 70s, this book is pared to the bone. It captures the rush of life, the flickering images, the buzzsaw riffs of living in the now and the twisting and turning takes of life in the modern times.

John Robb, May 2019

John Robb is a music journalist and commentator. He writes for, and runs, the Louder Than War website and Louder Than Words monthly music magazine. He has written several books on music including Punk Rock: An Oral History, Death to Trad Rock and The Nineties: What the Fuck Was All That About? and plays in both The Membranes and Goldblade.

Prologue

He lived by the sea, alone save for the birds that circled endlessly above his domain and the waves that had moulded and crushed the featureless coastline since the dawn of time. Alone and unloved, he needed no company; the multitude of imaginary sins that he called master and servant provided the burden that drove him onward and upward. A phoenix reborn from the ashes of mediocrity, the confining matter of his cerebellum held a fascination that bordered on addiction. The pattern of his existence had remained the same for fifteen years, the tightrope on which his peculiar insanity balanced stayed taut as he crossed from one side to the other, surefooted and determined. Underneath him the world disappeared and his safety net was cut away, a spinning useless facade that only reminded him of the life he had left behind an eternity before. As the sun rose, he trawled the beach searching for the debris that would set him free, chanting the mantras that kept the demons at bay. The devils that reality had sent to pursue him, unfaltering in their duty, their desperation exploiting his every weakness.

The gift promised him by the ocean would be his only as long as he remained vigilant. Alert and chaste, he rejected the temptations of the beast he had come to call society, the all-consuming monster he had battled since emerging. His answers waited for him somewhere beyond the horizon, gently drifting toward him, the patience of his quest a necessary evil if he was ever to reach his final destination.

9:42 P.M., August 28th 1998

"Hey Flanagan wake up. Come on man, fucking wake up."

"What…?"

"I said fucking wake up, it's time to shake it."

I'd always hated waking up in cars. The way your limbs always felt five times heavier than they actually were and that taste that always seemed to hang around inside your mouth, like you'd just swallowed the contents of an ashtray and chased the butts down with a pint of urine. It took me a couple of minutes to realise where I was, the clues coming together as I heard the relentless drone of the overworked windshield wipers and felt the incredible cramp that had started to crawl its way up my left leg. If there's one thing that's worse than waking up in a car, it's falling asleep in one knowing full well that you're going to feel like ten tons of shit when you eventually wake up. It's just the way of things, night becomes day, the seasons change and I fall asleep in cars. Maybe it's the gentle rocking motion that's always present on long road trips or it could just be the inane chatter of the boring fuckers I always seem to end up riding with. Personally, I prefer to think it's the former, but the sneaking suspicion that it's the later pops in there from time to time.

I wiped the sleep – funny how the names you associate with childhood stick with you through your adult life – from my eyes, stretched and turned to face Elliot, the cramp in my leg graduating from baby steps to star jumps.

"Where are we?"

"Some motorway service station."

This pissed me off. I wanted to be there and didn't want to be stuck miles from anywhere watching the Romanian National Circus as they stocked up on proteins and nutrients.

"What the fuck did you stop for?"

"Because we need to fill up, I need coffee and it's your turn to drive."

I looked at Elliot, sighed and reached over to grab my jacket from the back seat. As I struggled to pull the crumpled garment on, Elliot jumped out, slammed his door and made a mad dash for the shelter of the dimly lit complex that was covered in advertisements for a thousand and one varieties of fast food. Still half asleep, I followed his lead and stepped into the artificial lake that had gathered on the tarmac surface of the car park.

"Motherfucker!"

Swearing can be a release for all kinds of repressed emotion and can make you feel better about any bad situation, but this one was terminal and nothing short of a miracle would have fired my happy face. I trudged toward the nightmare that acted as a home away from home for wayward truckers, the rain rolling down my skin, jump-starting my senses letting normality wipe its feet on my doormat. The barrier was stiff, and being careful not to fall into the push me, pull me trap, I grasped the handle and swung it back. The stale air hit me like a tsunami and I knew what Tokyo must have felt like in all those old Godzilla movies. Overpowered, helpless and waiting for the end. I walked through the deserted corridors and entered the miserable slop house that tried to pass itself off as a restaurant. Elliot was seated at one of those moulded fibreglass tables that seem to grow straight out of the floor. I dutifully took my place opposite him and reached for the coffee that had cost roughly the same as a third world nation's annual gross national profit. It had been left to stew and fester for far too long and tasted bitter but provided welcome relief as it washed away my saliva – the saliva that had been replaced by Satan's semen while I slept.

Slouching back, Elliot grinned at me and began to speak.

"So, you're finally going back to the rat infested shit hole. Puts that promise you made into perspective doesn't it?"

"It's got fuck all to do with any promise I made." He laughed and tilted his head back.

One of those little habits he had that made me want to reach across and beat him until he gurgled like a brain dead newborn.

"Makes no difference to me. Another Flanagan promise flushed down the tubes. Admit it, you're home sick, you have to go back. No need to lose your rag."

Homesick. How could I be afflicted with homesickness if I hadn't even been back there in ten years? No, the only possible answer was that Elliot was talking shit and there was nothing new about that. Content in this belief, I relaxed and set my anxieties to one side.

"You don't know what the fuck you're talking about, which really doesn't surprise me."

There it was the anger that flashed across his face whenever someone challenged him. As quickly as it appeared, it was gone, and he continued his two-bit interrogation.

"Yeah? Then why else are you going back? It's not like there's anybody you want to see is there?"

His eyes narrowed as he hunted for a change in my demeanour, any change that would give him the advantage. Not this time you arrogant prick. I understood how his mind worked, how he tried to find a crack in your armour and when he located one, pecked at it until it splintered. I wasn't in the mood to hand him the satisfaction that came with victory.

"I just needed to get away from it for a while. I need to stimulate those creative juices, get them flowing again."

"That must be it. You'd hardly want to see that skank again would you?"

Fuck. I'd been played for a fool and froze like a rabbit caught in the headlights of an oncoming juggernaut.

"And which skank would that be Elliot?"

He had me. He knew it, and slid the hanged man across the table, tying the noose.

"Alison, the whore who fucked everyone except you. The one you used to have that thing for."

"You're kidding right? That's past history, all over with."

"If that's the case Flanagan, why have you got every video she's made? Why haven't you been able to have a normal relationship with any other woman? I'll tell you why, it's because you're still in love with her. No matter how hard you try to convince yourself that you're free of her, it never works. No woman will ever mean as much to you as she did and you'll never settle for second best. I feel for you Flanagan, I really do, you're my friend, but I'm warning you nothing good can come out of this childish infatuation of yours."

Some people will tell you that rejection is the hardest cross to bear. Me? I'd give it silver with defeat taking gold. Alison had ensured that I'd climbed the winner's podium and taken both medals in the relay. She'd made my teenage years tolerable. I'd lived to see her smile, hear her laugh and watch her glide through her traumas with the experience of a woman twice her age. Alison who had cried on my shoulder when every latest flame broke her heart. Each suitor had been the one – the one to live the nuclear family dream with. I used to comfort her, feel her hot breath erupt in twitching, whimpering fits against my neck and tell her that all men were bastards and she deserved so much more, whispering my reassurances whilst yearning to show her that I was the one, the one who would rip the heavens apart for that elusive chance to be with her. Alison, who sold her body to the camera, engaged in a fabrication of ecstasy with countless, nameless bodies, seeking the approval of one and all. Alison, the woman I'd sworn allegiance to ten years previously and was still in love with.

"Maybe you're right. But there's something else. I've been having the dreams again."

This shocked Elliot into fury. He slammed his coffee down and leaned across the table, stopping when our faces were level, four inches apart.

"You have got to be the dumbest Motherfucker I have ever met, and you know how many I have to deal with? Forget it, let it go, we fucked up and that's that. Get on with your life. We did it, we made it and you're still killing yourself with guilt. He was just a fucking wino who didn't mean shit to anyone. Fuck him, forget it, he's gone and unless there's some truth to the supernatural, he's not coming back. Man, I don't believe you. Do I look bothered by it? Do you think I let him ruin my dreams? Fuck no. Your problem Flanagan is that you live in the past and the sooner you get rid of all that crap that you carry around, the happier you'll be."

He was right, forget it, contract selective amnesia. Stumble around with my hands on my ears repeating 'La, La can't hear you. Can't be there I can't hear you'. I took a sip of the coffee, winced and said, "Yeah. Time to move on."

Elliot squeezed my arm, sat down and lit a cigarette. I stared at him as he gradually exhaled.

"Fucking right it's time to move on. I don't want to hear another word about it, understand? If you want to go down, that's your business, but I'm not going with you. You got it?"

"I got it." It felt like the words had come from someone else, someone standing behind me.

"Finally." Elliot stood, stubbed out his cigarette and turned to make his way to the door. "Here's the keys, start her up, I gotta go piss."

I picked the keys up and headed out to the car and the perpetual rain.

10:17 P.M. August 28th 1998

Rental cars stick to the rulebook written by a government department like flies to a three day carcass, resolute in their determination to justify public spending. Any vehicle that violates these suggestions can be tried by the inquisition that awaits all heretics at the scrap yard. The gears have to crunch, it has to creak and groan every time you take a bend, and be totally unresponsive below sixty miles per hour. Once you've adjusted to departmental regulations, you should be able to find a level at which man and machine can co-operate and at least appear to function together. The whole notion of perfect harmony was a bullshit slogan dreamt up by a bored executive sipping a Margarita, three under par at the fifteenth hole of his country club. Tired of bureaucratic policy, I came up with a rule of my own. As long as the stereo works, you can deal with all the other shit adversity hurls at you. Check the damn thing before you leave the garage, you don't know who had the car before you or what they could have been up to. I read the papers. I watch television. I know the depraved way sales representatives behave. If there's a hole in something, they'll fuck it. Stick their dicks in, wiggle the toothpicks around and shoot their loads. No mess, no fuss. Missed your quarterly target? Don't worry, yank your fly down, flop the old boy out and get to work. Better luck next time.

   Driving tends to focus certain areas of your mind and let others run free and so I found myself hurtling down the motorway while Elliot slept, oblivious to the Black Flag tape that was eating the stereo from the inside. Drifting back and forth, I finally allowed my mind to claw its way back toward my childhood. I'd grown up in a small tourist dependent town whose population consisted of retired half dead couples and the families of the bastions of industry who had been relocated by corporations – whose power was absolute. I was a normal, everyday, maladjusted kid from another dysfunctional family. I went to school. I did okay considering how much shit I took and got the fuck out before having to grab a rifle and target the sitting ducks that littered the area like a termite infestation. Acquaintances came and went and I guess I only had five real friends. Saying we were tight would have sold the whole deal short and understated the case. We needed and fed off each other; devouring the nourishment that each gave to the others willingly. Boiling the flesh away, grinding the bones to dust until all that remained was a colourless soup catalysed by bonding. It was like one of those Italian family recipes that only Mama and her secret ingredient could produce. Sometimes you'd stumble across it, but more often than not, Mama would take her speciality with her to the grave. Elliot and Alison had both been in the selective grouping I had called friends. My father had described Elliot as being full of enthusiasm but lacking talent, which was no big deal seeing as my dad defined 'talent' as the ability to strip an internal combustion engine, blindfolded, with one hand tied behind your back, racing against the clock. Anything more than ten minutes was wholly unacceptable. I'd always hung out with Elliot, mainly because he was the only kid who took more shit than I did. I knew that if I stuck close, the Hitler Youth would spare me and concentrate their efforts on him. I wish the others had made the same kind of impression on me as Elliot and Alison had, but ten years is a long time to try and store images in limited cognitive space. They're easily replaced.

I couldn't forget meeting Alison – that's a memory I cherish. My erstwhile partner, Elliot had told me that he knew a girl who didn't mind playing 'Doctors' and if you showed her your parts (it's just the way these things come back to you) she'd return the favour. I was hooked from the moment she dropped her panties and have been ever since. Becky, Blake and Taylor came along and just seemed to hang around and our group established, nobody and nothing could come between us because when you're that close, there's no secrets that you can hold onto or hide. I managed to keep one for eight years and still wonder how things might have been if I'd held on to it.

I had watched him, on and off, for eight years using his madness as a yardstick to measure my own sanity. I'd laughed, pulled faces and thrown stones at him for no other reason than the infantile pursuits that filled my days had grown cold and tedious. Lacking imagination and having a low tolerance for boredom had exposed me to the role of tormentor. It wasn't until I had suffered similar pain at the hands of other equally bored children that I began to understand the concept of being broken both mentally and physically. I watched new generations persecute him, an outsider due to the self-obsession and introversion that occupies all teenagers. Never once did his faith desert him as he retired to lick his wounds and returned to the fray, day after day. His belief in his own destiny strengthened him as the old world burned in the fires of Babylon.

One of the advantages of living in a small town, or disadvantages depending on your point of view, is that everyone knows exactly what you're up to. There are no concealed truths between the coffee mornings and wife swapping parties and I started to piece together the fragments of gossip that occasionally came my way, about the stranger on the beach. According to whichever story was most popular at the time, he was either a war hero, an esteemed physics professor who had cracked under the strain or an escaped mental patient responsible for serving up his family as tasty breakfast treats. This wasn't enough, the only way to solve the greatest mystery of the twentieth century was to go undercover and investigate him, probe him, talk to him and find out for myself.

I can still remember that summer with crystal clarity. While other fourteen year old boys were trying to charm fourteen year old girls out of their knickers, I listened to his stories. His tales of the Illuminati, the fallibility of space exploration, why George Segal was the Anti-Christ and how the coming Armageddon would shape the Earth for mankind's successor, the arachnid, fascinated me. The more fantastic his stories became and the more involved he became in telling them, the more I had to listen. The cliff-hangers submerged me in his universe, one that was free of complications and abstract ties. If I'd managed to keep my mouth shut four years later, the memory might still be a precious moment of a forgotten childhood and I wouldn't have helped to drown his stories in a river of blood on a humid July evening. That's the problem with recalling your past; you can't separate the good from the bad. Oh sure, I've heard stories about hypnosis and counselling helping the wounded victims of nefarious deeds, but short of brain stem cauterisation or a full frontal lobotomy the baggage stays with you and doesn't go missing en-route. At the end of the day, it all comes down to whether or not you can live with yourself, whether you can look in the mirror, strike a pose and step out into the rat race or open your wrists with a straight razor and hitch a ride to oblivion. I've always envied those who can lie for a living, the go-getters who can wink at you while sticking a knife in your back and twisting the blade. The minority who could steal the leprechaun's gold and convince them that they only had the little people's best interests at heart. Unfortunately, it's envy born out of frustration. I was always the one who got caught, the one the authority figures singled out.

Every kid likes to think that they can outsmart the man, those in a position of power, forgetting that twenty years previously the man thought exactly the same way. It's one of the failings of youth – bravado versus experience. For those in power it's like shooting fish in a barrel. In their eyes all juveniles are guilty of something; it's just a matter of establishing the degree of guilt. They can smell fear and read it like a cheap detective novel. Teachers, cops – different titles – but they're all after the same thing. Compliance and order at any cost. Five minutes with them and my palms would start to sweat; the confessions would start rolling, putting me in the frame for all kinds of twisted shit.

This brought its own advantages though. If I was busted, nobody else would be caught. Don't take that the wrong way, it wasn't out of some warped sense of honour that I didn't turn anyone else in. At the time I'd have done anything to get them to stop. Truth is, I panicked and couldn't focus on anything except confessing. It makes me laugh when I think of the fraudulent persona that was built around me. I was the one the pigs couldn't grind down, the one who kept his mouth shut and stayed cool. Ice cold to the core, a legend in the locality. Only the police knew the truth and I wasn't about to blow a good thing for neither love nor money.

That was how we grew up, my friends pulling all the crap and me spending everyone's share of the time in a ten by eight. Mostly we had fun, we argued and made up, discovered all the things teenagers aren't supposed to do, but do anyway. Alcohol, drugs, sex and rock and roll. Elliot and I dove headlong into punk rock while the others grabbed at whatever fashion happened to be passing through the fickle hands of the teen magazine editors. The only constant was our friendship and love for one another. That couldn't be bought off or chipped away and it was all we needed to wade through the quagmire of small town life.

Things went the way they always had, cruising past, until that summer we left school. The world was out there, slumbering, and all we wanted to do was to get out there and wake it up. Make our mark and leave an impression that nobody would forget in a hurry. Becky, Blake, Alison and Taylor were all headed for university. I'd taken a year out after Elliot had convinced me that the band we were playing in, Crack Jester, was going to smash the system and change the way music was listened to and thought about. He didn't need the education trip, as he put it. It was another four years of school designed to make you a model citizen and a way of purging any rebellious instincts. Motherfucker could have told me anything and I've have followed without hesitating. Since we were kids he's always had that effect on people, a fatal charm that drew you to him and made you finish what he'd started. Nobody ever showed Elliot how to do anything they did it for him. I've seen him work that cold magic a hundred thousand times and it never fails to send a shiver down my spine. I honestly thought that there wasn't anything that could separate us. Naivety can overcome a lot of things but there's one compelling force that it doesn't stand a chance against. Self-preservation.

I guess it came to a head on one of those evenings that make the perfect setting for a post card. The sun had dropped on its axis; its heat lingering despite a clear sky and a sea breeze that rolled gently over you and blew sweet kisses in your ear. To be different we'd spent the afternoon knocking back six packs of Moosehead and smoking blunts, talking shit to while away the hours.

Hell, at that age you've got an eternity of empty days in front of you and don't care what the future brings, as long as it brings something. Anything to bridge the void that had suddenly opened up. I don't know who suggested it, no, wait it was Becky, I'm pretty sure it was Becky; the idea was there and that was all that mattered. Hey, why not reveal that one skeleton that everyone has, the one they keep locked away in the deepest, darkest corner of their soul. Think of it as a bonding exercise, then no matter how far we travelled or where we ended up, we'd always be close. All you had to do was close your eyes and the others would be there. Always. What I didn't know then and now know only too well, is that when you close your eyes you never know what's going to be there waiting for you.

My parents used to delight in telling me that I was an open book, and that what you see is what you get. Why hadn't I told my friends about the stranger on the beach? Maybe because it was mine, it was too personal, too valuable to share. Or maybe I was scared that they'd tear my carefully constructed image to shreds. Whatever the reason, it was the only thing I had left that they didn't have. My turn came too quickly.

"Come on Flanagan, share," said Blake, handing me the remnants of a joint as he spoke.

"Uh, alright. If you laugh, I swear to God I'll fucking kill you." I still believed in God back then. You move on though and I've seen too much to still believe in paradise and a cavalcade of angels.

"What makes you think we'd laugh at you Flanagan?" asked Becky, fluttering her eyelashes as she stared across at me.

The laughter was infectious – it encouraged and relaxed me. These people were my friends, if I couldn't tell them, whom could I reveal my folly to?

"You know that old guy who hangs around the beach?" I began slowly.

"The lunatic who killed his family," nodded Taylor, draining another beer. I could have left it there, made some excuse about being cut off and if Taylor

12

knew so much about the guy, why didn't he just fucking carry on, filling in the blanks as he saw fit.

"Yeah, that guy." I forced the words through clenched teeth, glaring at Taylor who threw his hands up in a gesture of mock defence. If he hadn't pissed me off, I might have found the act hilarious. I breathed in, held it, exhaled and continued.

"Well, you all know the stories about him right? It's the kind of shit your folks used to try and scare you with when you wouldn't do as you were told. You know if you don't eat your greens the bogeyman of the sea will get you and there's nothing we'll be able to do about him?" I picked up a fresh beer, snapped the ring pull, raised it to my mouth and took a swallow. "They had the opposite effect on me, and I had to find out what the real deal was with him."

"What is your fucking malfunction Flanagan? They were just stories," Elliot chipped in, fumbling as he tried to roll a joint.

"Whatever. The point is, I followed the fucker and found out what I needed to." I'd be lying if I said I was anything less than smug.

Something ignited in Alison's eyes, and I could have sworn it was concern.

"He could have done anything to you. Killed you and left your body for the tide. I wish you'd think about some of your ridiculous ideas for more than five seconds," she snapped.

This made me blush, turn scarlet as all the feelings that I'd kept suppressed, rushed to the surface.

"So what did you find out?" whispered Becky. Curiosity had got the better of her, the joint in her fingers burning down to the roach.

"Nothing much. He's just a harmless nutter who likes to tell stories," I replied, shrugging my shoulders.

"What kind of stories?" asked Blake, excitedly moving forward to ensure he didn't miss any details.

"Not the kind you're thinking of. I told you, he's harmless," I laughed.

Blake had loved horror movies; those gore flicks that used to line the shelves of video rental stores in the early eighties in particular. The possibility that he might hear firsthand tales of evisceration, dismemberment and decapitation was almost more than he could bear. My answer disappointed him and deflated, he sat back.

"No, they were like...shit, how can I put this?" I hadn't thought this far ahead. I'd convinced myself that they wouldn't be interested and would dismiss my account as bullshit before I'd even finished my opening sentence.

"People are getting old here Flanagan," said Elliot.

"Alright, fuck, keep cool. They're the kind of demented ramblings that get you a first class ticket to the nuthouse. He probably lost his happy pills," I offered, hoping that this would steer them away from me.

"And that's it, is it Flanagan? That's the great secret you've been hiding all this time? Some psycho forgot to take his medication. There's got to be more to it than that, or are you really that fucking boring?" Elliot again. He continued, "What made you hang around to listen?"

If sarcasm truly is the lowest form of humour, then Elliot had definitely missed out on that lesson. Humiliation was his favourite pastime and the worse he made you feel, the more he enjoyed it.

"Yeah, they were pretty bizarre, but there was this edge to them. They made me want to feel what he was feeling and I wanted to know what he knew." It was the only explanation I could give. There was no way I could translate the myriad of colours and sights that his stories had awakened within me.

"Do you think he'd tell us a story?" asked Elliot slyly.

"What do you mean?" The tone of the conversation was starting to make me feel uncomfortable. This was wrong. All wrong.

"Do you think he'd tell us a story?" repeated Elliot.

"Why?" I put my beer down and stared at the ground. The loose cigarette papers curled as the air from the ocean flowed over them.

"If they're as good as you're making them out to be, I want to hear one, that's all." The pitch of his voice had changed and this worried me. No one else seemed to have noticed.

"Oh man, yeah. I've got to hear one of these stories. Do you think he'd tell us one Flanagan? Do you?" gurgled Blake.

"I don't know. People freak him out. I don't even know if we'd be able to find him." I was desperate to get out of this situation. I wanted to avoid it, make it go away. Why did we have to play the stupid fucking game?

"But he knows you Flanagan, so that shouldn't be a problem. Besides, if we can't find him, we can't find him. There's no harm in looking is there?" asked Elliot, reading the label on the side of his can.

What could happen? The chances of us finding him were remote and if we did, they'd listen to his psychobabble and go back to drinking. I regained my composure and dispelled the nausea that was swirling around my stomach.

"I guess not. Let's go."

Descending to the beach from our vantage point on the cliffs high above seemed to take forever. As we climbed down, I thought about the old man and prayed that we wouldn't find him. There was something about our new adventure that filled me with dread. A silent terror, that nudged me when I tried to reason with it and refused to let go when I tried to ignore it. I centred on what bothered me about Elliot's plan. Jealousy. I didn't want to share with the other children. I wanted to keep the temple I'd built to house my collection of fables guarded within my mind. I wanted to be the sole patron, the only one who could come and go as he pleased, reassured by their presence and satisfied by their generosity. If the collection was broken up and distributed amongst us, their value would decrease. The misery that defiled the world around me would tarnish them and shatter the picture of innocence I had frozen in time. My reflection would stare back at me from a thousand different angles.

The footholds that littered the face of the cliff reached out to support and guide me, their hard tendrils comforting me, easing my journey, helping me reach my destination. My feet sank into the damp sand, its suction increased by the moisture it held, a gift left by the departing tide. I dusted myself off and looked around. The others had gathered in a semi-circle twenty feet to the right.

"Where to now Flanagan?" asked Alison.

"This way." I turned to my left and followed the trail that I had committed to memory four years before. To an outsider, all coastlines look the same, their barren likeness stretching out, empty and unwelcoming. It takes years to truly know a place. I could have been waving a white cane and I still wouldn't have put a foot wrong or made a wrong turn. I cursed the clarity that drew me onward, ever onward to his home, his shelter, his refuge.

He sat with his back to us, crouching in front of a fire, rocking back and forth on his haunches, his muttering impotent and handicapped as it competed with the roar of the ocean. If he was aware of our presence, he didn't show it.

"What now Flanagan?" said Blake quickly, desperately trying to disguise the excitement in his voice.

"I don't know." Why was he here? Why couldn't he have been looking for crap at the tide line?

"What did you do when you came here?" hissed Elliot, my apparent idiocy pushing him to boiling point.

"I used to just walk over, sit down and let him do the rest," I replied.

"Sounds like a plan to me," he said, rushing toward the mouth of the cave, the others trailing him.

I've been over and over what happened next. I've tried to rationalise it, attempted to make sense of the nonsensical, using logic against the chaos that filtered through the fabric of structure, but was defeated by superior forces every time I replayed it. My mentor turned, screamed, grabbed a pebble and hurled it at Elliot. The projectile found its mark and struck Elliot above his right eye, opening his brow.

Elliot grunted, stumbled and fell to his knees, his hands flying to his face before he hit the ground. I saw him pull his hands away, staring incredulously at the fluid, the crimson fluid that oozed between his fingers. Everything slowed down, just seemed to decelerate. Elliot rose to his feet and ran at his protagonist shouting, his speed increasing with every step.

"You cunt! You fucking prick! You want to fight; I'll show you how to fight!"

The old man screamed again and curled himself into a ball as Elliot drew closer. The air became a thick mucus that was difficult to breathe. My jaw opened and closed, mouthing the warning that never came. I heard a thud as the story teller's body leapt up, heard a crack that reminded me of leather being snapped and watched Elliot stand over him, kicking for all he was worth, each blow echoed and amplified by the rear of the crude dwelling. Blake and Taylor materialised from nowhere, grabbed Elliot and yanked him backwards, his feet lashing out at the empty space his target had once occupied. I stood, planted in the sand that was sucking at my boots, rooted to the spot by the dread that had re-emerged and surged through me augmented by what I had witnessed.

"Oh God. Oh God. Oh God! Oh fuck, what have you done, what have you done?" screamed Taylor. He was crying.

"You've fucking killed him," whispered Blake, pointing at the carcass that lay spreadeagled against the wall.

"Fuck him, prick got what he deserved. He's not dead, are you old man? Fucker's faking it because he doesn't want to get some more," Elliot said as he shook himself loose from Taylor and Blake.

"You want some more? Answer me Motherfucker. You want some more?" snapped Elliot, tapping the prone figure with the side of his boot. Those big fucking white Hi Tech boots he always wore.

The colour drained from his face, the tapping slowed down as he realised that his words were falling on deaf ears.

"Oh Jesus. We're fucked."

I became aware of a faint noise, a humming that was gradually getting louder and louder. It suddenly erupted and all hell broke loose. Alison held Becky at the entrance to the cave, Blake, Taylor and Elliot stood inside, just to the left of the fire, but I couldn't hear what they were saying, couldn't distinguish one voice from another. The choir of the damned spoke, its wailing sighs cleared the fog that had enveloped me and forced the air back into my lungs. I felt my stomach contract, its contents exploded from my nose and mouth, hitting the sand as a million multi-coloured raindrops. My hands were shaking and a dark stain was spreading across the front of my jeans. I staggered toward Elliot, it wasn't cold but my hands still shook. He was white and I could see the flames dancing in his eyes, illuminating the tears that followed the contours of his nose. I stared at my obsession and watched as the liquid leaking from his sockets began to circumvent the remnants of his skull. I laughed. Laughed and laughed, heard the sound bounce between the cave and my piss stained, vomit soaked body and carried on laughing.

Death hadn't been part of my agenda before the lights went out for the final time on the curiosity that I had come to know and in some strange way, even love. Sure, I'd known that it existed, after all life in the eighties had turned it into an entertainment spectacular. You only had to name your poison and you were free to load up on it until your brain turned to mush and your organs burst. The choices were infinite and variety was no longer a privilege reserved solely for the rich. It became a commodity that was bought and sold, the stocks floated and the shareholders rewarded with holiday homes and recreational vehicles. Leisure activities were controlled and monopolised by the Grim Reaper. The cloak and scythe had been replaced by an Armani suit and a personal organiser. Modernisation was the key word and aggressive corporate takeovers dominated the reports that were piled six high on the desk of the chairman of the board, Lucifer.

It was all a game, the longer you played, the greater the risk. If you had a bad day at the office, you put your feet up, took a peak at that snuff movie from Hong Kong, chopped yourself a couple of lines on the bathroom mirror and broke out those new toiletries. Safety was paramount; the company had already tested their products on students, homeless children in Brazil and fluffy bunnies. What's that, you wanted a guarantee? Nothing in life was guaranteed, you should have read the small print, paragraph three, sub section seven, and there it was; built in obsolescence. Don't think, get out the door, hit a couple of bars and pick up a willing partner. Forget your condoms? Infection was over dramatised, something that happened to the other guy. Besides it was a real turn on, spin the chamber and bite down hard on the barrel. One in six, the odds were in your favour, everything was a gamble. Industries rose and fell as they chased the consumers' desire to immerse themselves in fantasy. Escapism became the route of all evil, the prisoners of war tunnelling further and further as the chairman took all bets and shot dice with his minions. The board met twice a week to pin the tail on the donkey and pluck their victims' souls. As the wheels turned, the pursuit of pleasure became a vicious circle whose tracks you rode at your own peril. But the rush, the incredible rush, was well worth the price of admission. Generation X became desensitised to the great equaliser, the homologous entity that didn't discriminate. All were welcome, all races, sexes, creeds and classes.

I was aware of death's presence, but wasn't prepared for its reality. When my time came, I thought it would be swift, the dark angel visiting me as I slept; incontinence and senility protecting my soul from the ice embrace the winged apparition used as its calling card. The thought that the spring on my internal clock could unwind or snap at any time scared the holy crap out of me, and the sudden dawning of this knowledge loosened the chord that suspended the Sword of Damocles above me. In that brief moment, I questioned all I had been taught. What of the Nirvana that was supposed to follow a peaceful death and pretty flowers? Did heaven wait for me or was I going to burn for all eternity? It was this fear of the unknown that that made me laugh; if you didn't laugh, you might as well give in. Punch your card on the way out and accept your gift for years of service without complaint.

"Oh Jesus, we're fucked."

I had to stop laughing, had to hold on to anything I could, establish my grip and cling to it or be cast adrift on the sea of madness. I thought about my mother's exercise videos and the breathing techniques that the former beauty queen presenters used in order to prepare themselves for the punishing aerobic regimes. In, count to twenty, out, slow exhale, feel the blood begin to oxygenate and the muscles absorb the energy.

"Shut up," I whispered.

"Oh Jesus Christ, we are fucking screwed."

"Shut the fuck up," I screamed, grabbing at Elliot's collar. I pinned him against the wall of the cave. "Shut the fuck up."

Once. I've only lost my temper with Elliot once. Oh, he's pushed me far enough since, but I've always laughed it off, kept calm and remembered the exercises. When you're being fed crap it's easier to force it down with a shit eating grin plastered on your face, which implies you're enjoying each morsel. It annoys the hell out of people and that's the point. Act like you don't give a fuck.

Elliot stared down at me, his tears mixing with the snot that was bubbling on his upper lip.

"Oh Jesus, we're fucked," he whined. He sounded pinched and his voice had a nasal quality that I usually associated with supermarket managers.

"No, you're fucked. Did you see anyone else hit him? I don't think so," I said, increasing the pressure I held him with. He squirmed and I pushed harder.

"What...?" Bewildered, his voice trailed off.

"I said you're fucked. You hit him, you killed him. Not Becky, not Blake, not Taylor, not Alison, not me; just you. You did it all by yourself."

I opened my hands and he started to slide down. His jacket caught on the jagged rocks that protruded from the wall. He wriggled and half ripped one of the patches he'd sewn on it with an antique sewing machine that was powered by a pedal you hit with your foot. The faster you hit the pedal, the faster the machine would go.

"I didn't mean to do it...he started it..." he spluttered, looking at us, searching for sympathy.

The well had run dry.

"Yeah, the judge is really going to believe that. I'm sorry your honour, I didn't mean to do it, it just happened. I'd been smoking and drinking and just blew. That's really convincing Elliot. He'll hang you by your balls," I said, shaking my head.

"What is wrong with the pair of you? A man's been killed and all you can think about is yourselves. What about him?" Becky said, pushing Alison away as she walked towards us.

She'd made her point. We were arguing about legal proceedings while a body lay battered and beaten on the ground, its blood flowing across the surface of the rocks, forming pools which spilled over to start the process again.

"We could throw him in the sea," said Blake quietly.

"Excuse me?" said Becky, facing him as she spoke, unsure of what he had just suggested.

"I saw it in a film. We throw him in the sea and when the tide comes in, it'll bash him against the rocks. No one will ever know the difference," explained Blake.

"Or Elliot could just go to the police and turn himself in. This isn't one of your fucking video nasties Blake, it's the real world. We're stuck with a body and you're off taking a trip in dreamland," she shouted at him.

"It wasn't a video nasty. It was Columbo or another one of those cop shows. It worked in that," he answered, offended by the accusation she'd levelled at him.

"I don't care what show it was and if it worked or not. Columbo and television are make believe. The police investigate things here. Nobody gets away with murder. They'll get us and we'll end up in jail," Becky replied as though she was trying to explain algebra to chimpanzees.

"That's right; we'll all go to jail. At least we will if I go to the police," said Elliot, nervously lighting a joint.

Everyone turned to face him. He was calm. Too calm.

"The way I see it is like this. If I go to the police, it'll be my word against yours. The truth won't matter, they'll charge us all." His words were soft, slow and methodical. "I say we try Blake's plan and see what happens."

"You'd do that? You'd turn us all in?" This shit was not happening to me. It was not happening.

"Look, I don't want to go to prison, you don't want to go to prison. What's the alternative? Blake's idea is the only way out," he said, flicking the ash from the joint on the floor.

"But I didn't do anything. I only wanted to hear a story," sobbed Alison.

"Oh please, do you think the police care? They'll lock you away just like that." Elliot said, snapping his thumb and forefinger together.

"They won't believe you," I whispered.

"No, of course they won't. But they'll believe an honest citizen like you won't they Flanagan? Face it; they've had you in so many times, you've become a permanent feature, part of the decor. What makes you think that they'd listen to any of you? I'm telling you, they get me, they get all of us," he retorted, his confidence growing with every syllable.

"There's a word for what you're doing Elliot..." began Taylor.

"Oh, uh, let me guess. Would that be blackmail?" Sarcasm and confidence. He was good, I'll give him that. "No, you're doing a favour for a friend. Offering him a hand up when he's down."

"Actually," Taylor corrected him, "the word I was going use is shitty. You don't give a fuck about any of us do you?"

Elliot shrugged. "What's it going to be?"

How does that saying go? The things you see when you've left your gun at home. I should have taken my chances with the law and walked away. They knew me. They knew that I didn't have the balls to even bend the rules. I was a voyeur, not a perpetrator. A reluctant accomplice who got a look in now and again. There it was. The phrase that determined the outcome. Accomplice. Go along with the plan or risk getting shanked in the showers by multiple rapists. I took a minute to study the extensive list of options.

"You really are a scheming two faced cunt aren't you Elliot? What choice do we have?" I said, bowing my head.

"Sticks and stones may break my bones Flanagan, but the man will never get me," he replied, and smiled at me.

"Excuse me for interrupting the boys only meeting, but are the rest of you really going to go along with this insanity?" asked Becky.

I nodded and so did Taylor. Alison still stood at the mouth of the cave crying and Blake looked like someone had just stolen his favourite toy.

"It's a fucking good idea. I don't see any of you thinking your way out," he grumbled.

"You want another option? Fine, try this one. Any of us could go to the police and tell them what he did," snapped Becky, pointing at Elliot.

This intrigued Elliot and he met her stare, head on. She didn't falter or try to break his gaze. She dug her heels in and prepared for war. He shook his head, looked at the roof of the cave and relaxed even further.

"Becky, Becky, Becky. Same old story. You tell them what I did and as soon as they arrest me, I'll tell them it was you. Think about what you're saying. The police always prefer the easy answer, there's less paperwork. They'll charge us all and close the case. Tell them anything and you're admitting that you were involved," he laughed.

She considered what Elliot had said, running her fingers through her hair as she nodded in reluctant agreement.

"What about the blood?" Alison had stopped crying. Her voice was devoid of emotion and had become hard and precise.

"What...?" asked Elliot incredulously, amazed that anyone would try to throw a rod into the spokes of the master plan. Damn the proletariat.

"What about the blood? It's everywhere. He lived in this cave, so the tide won't come up this far. It won't wash it away. What about the blood? What are we going to do about the blood? As soon as they find the body, they're bound to come up here. What are we going to do about the blood?" she continued, focusing on Elliot.

"I...I don't know." Fear was cutting at his newfound confidence, it turned full circle and took him right back to the beginning.

"I know what to do," said Blake "it's easy. Roll the body up in one of the blankets, carry it to the sea, unwrap it and dump it. The blood is even easier. We take his rags, wipe all the shit up, fill them with rocks, find a cave that the tide will reach and throw them in the pools there. No trace, simple," he was pleased with himself.

That much was evident. I guess I'd never considered the possibility that you could learn anything constructive from slasher flicks, but there it was. How to cover your tracks.

"Okay. Flanagan and Taylor, you're the biggest, you do the body and the rest of us will get to work in here, cleaning this shit up. Come on, the sooner we can get it done, the sooner we can get the fuck out of here." Elliot was back in control and rallied his rag tag army, hoping against hope that this suicidal charge would be enough to clear the finishing posts.

Wrapping the body wasn't as hard as I'd thought it would be. It was just like rolling up a carpet. That was the only way to get through it. Just rolling a carpet, just discarding rubbish, throwing out the trash, no sweat, no problem. I kept my eyes closed because I knew his dead pupils were staring at me, pleading with me, trying to persuade me to change my mind. No way muchacho, I'm just throwing out the trash. If I couldn't see him, he wasn't there. On the count of four, we both lifted and walked out of the cave toward the ocean. Death increases the weight of a body, adds at least twenty pounds and trying to maintain your hold on a carcass is next to impossible. A coffin would have provided a medium to balance the mass, brass handles to grip and focus on. Blankets were never meant to serve as body bags and as we slipped and slid across the rocks, our load swung between us like a lead hammock, constantly changing its centre of gravity. I was waiting for a vigilant fisherman to spot us, see our grisly cargo, turn us in and sell his story to the Sunday tabloids. The fish weren't biting and we pressed on, the loneliness of our morbid journey consuming my thoughts and actions. Taylor tried to make small talk, his way of passing the time, but I couldn't hear or understand him. I was discarding rubbish, throwing out the trash. Just doing my chores before dinner. It took almost an hour to reach an outcrop that was high enough for us to dispose of our package. Taylor jerked the trailing edge of the blanket and the body flopped out. Its strings cut, the mannequin stopped abruptly as it struck the ground.

"No more dancing for you Marionette." I giggled. Taylor looked at me blankly as he folded the blanket, laid it to one side and spoke.

"You grab hold of his feet and I'll take his arms. I'll count to three and we heave him out there okay?"

"Okay. Throwing out the trash on the count of three. Don't look so sad clown, we're all going to be washed up eventually," I said, smiling at the old friend who lay in front of me.

"Flanagan? Are you okay Flanagan?" Taylor sounded worried.

"Yeah, I'm fine. Just saying goodbye," I answered, "do you think we should say a prayer or sing a hymn?"

"I'm not in the mood for singing Flanagan but don't let me stop you. Let's get on with it and get out of here. Ready?" he asked pulling the outstretched arms upwards. I nodded, lifted the feet and started to hum 'Amazing Grace'.

"One .Two. Three," shouted Taylor.

The body hung momentarily in the air and then spiralled down, turning and twisting as it fell. I thought the splash would have been bigger, an event I could have graded with scorecards, but the entry was flawed and far from the perfect ten that I felt obliged to award him. He bobbed up, once, twice, then disappeared below the waves as they smashed into the base of the cliff. I said a silent prayer, shivered, picked up the blanket and lit a cigarette.

"That's that then. A burial at sea," I said to Taylor.

"Yeah, I guess so," he replied, peering down at the water, searching for a trace of the deposit we had made. He stepped back. "Time we were going Flanagan, the others will be wondering where we are. You want me to take care of that?" he asked, indicating the blanket.

"No, that's alright. I got it." I carefully placed the folded blanket inside my jacket and fastened the zipper.

We covered the distance to our starting point in half the time it had taken us to reach the cliffs. Maybe what they say is true. Half the fun is in getting there. On the way back we talked and talked, discussed politics, sex and music, talked about anything except our disposal duty. Somehow it didn't seem right. Leave the dead to rest in peace, let bygones be bygones. The others were waiting for us by the cave. Under Elliot's guidance they'd made swift work of the spring cleaning. There was nothing left to indicate that anyone had even been there. Behind them the fire still burned, projecting and enlarging their shadows. Elliot strolled towards us, his hands in his pockets.

"Everything okay?" he asked casually.

"Uh huh. Whoever finds him will think that he took a high dive off the cliffs," I answered.

"Makes you wonder what goes through the minds of some of these lunatics doesn't it. Sure, he was weird but who would've thought that he'd have committed suicide like that? Such a damn waste," sighed Elliot.

"Yeah, that's right, you keep telling yourself that," said Becky, unable to disguise her disgust. "I'm going home. I've had more than enough excitement for one night."

"See you around," Elliot replied, staring at her as she headed for the beach. Alison, Blake and Taylor followed without saying a word, fading into the descending darkness. I was left alone with Elliot.

"You coming?"

I shook my head. "No, I'm going to hang around here for a while. Got a lot of thinking to do." He approached me cautiously. "You're not going to, you know, do anything stupid are you?"

I smiled. "Don't worry Elliot; I just need to clear my head."

"Alright Flanagan. Give me a call tomorrow?"

"Sure."

I sat by the fire, watching as the darkness swallowed Elliot and waited. Satisfied that he was finally gone, I undid my jacket, removed the blanket and spread it out on the floor of the cave. I stared at it and tried to interpret the patterns that had been left by the congealing blood. In the light of the open flames they writhed, snarled and dragged me into a world of surreal visual landscapes and prophecies. The crimson stains separated, became elemental colours that illustrated and suspended the boundaries of mortality; the spirit guides that unravelled the plains of existence and revealed the secrets that had been hidden from humanity. I understood.

The afterlife was an illusion. Heaven was a safeguard used and exploited by religion and hell was life on Earth. A life limited to hopeless struggle, suffering, isolation, misery and misfortune. There was nothing to hold onto, no straws to clutch at. Death was the only salvation, the only freedom that any of us would truly know. The retirement that promised nothing and took everything in return, the cosmic joke whose punch line was delayed only by time. I felt my old friend's essence as it bound itself to me and unlocked the gate to a cage of self-loathing. The beginning of the symbiotic relationship that would dominate my days, manipulate my nights and strip away my dignity. The warmth of the fire provided security, the return to the womb I longed for and I crawled under the blanket and fell asleep, haunted by dreams of redemption. I still don't know how long I slept in the cave, but as I made my way home, the blanket folded inside my jacket, the sun crept above the horizon and created a dull yellow pathway that I followed to my front door. I picked up a bottle of milk, pushed my thumb through its delicate silver top and drank, sucking the nurturing liquid down, ignoring the excess as it rolled down my neck, inside my shirt and merged with the dried blood that had impregnated the shroud I clutched to my heart. I walked into my bedroom and took my jacket off. The blanket was soft and I caressed it as I removed the bottom drawer of my bedside cabinet. I positioned it carefully inside the unit, replaced the drawer, turned on the television and began to flick through the channels with the remote control.

The summer drifted lazily past us and became almost a non-event. There were parties, all the usual teenage delinquency, but it wasn't the same. Something else had died that night and we saw less and less of each other. We didn't talk about him – we didn't need to. Every time we looked into each other's eyes the entire scenario unfolded. I remember reading the local paper after the body had been discovered by an elderly couple, two days after it had gone swimming. He made frontpage news. Accidental death the police called it. Agatha Christie would have seen right through it. One by one they left our small town behind as they searched for some new meaning to help fulfil their dreams and ambitions. I stuck with Elliot playing punk rock, and my friends? They all vanished, choosing a different path. Each night as I lay in bed, I held the blanket close and thought about the old man, wondering if anyone else thought about him. Wondering if anyone missed him the way I did.

11:41 P.M. August 28th, 1998

Rolling back into town wasn't quite the extravaganza that I'd thought it would be. Sometimes, when you've been away from a place for too long your mind plays tricks on you. It mixes your memories up until all that's left is a mass of confusion. I tried to remember the places that had meant something to me as we sped past them. Names and faces, nothing came. All I could see was the old man's body floating in the ocean. I fumbled for the electric window release, stabbing at it until I heard the familiar whine of the motors kick in and the glass rolled down. Relaxing into my seat, I inhaled deeply and immediately started to gag. It was still there. The stench of human decay that was present, below the candyfloss and cooking fat that poured from the takeaways that lined the coastline. It was the smell of a population waiting to die. I yanked the steering wheel to one side, slammed on the brakes, fell out of the car door, on to my knees and brought up the coffee I'd swallowed on the motorway. My vision started to blur as my stomach muscles strained to empty all that they could. The tears ran down my face and joined the mess that had appeared on the pavement.

I spat and decided to stay where I was, take some time to get used to the foul, rancid air that welcomed families and thrived on joy. Eventually the nausea passed and I returned to the car. Elliot was still asleep. Sliding the car into gear, I pulled out and continued towards Elliot's family home. I drove past the hotels and amusement arcades that acted as a windbreaker for the rest of the town. They hadn't changed. The paint was still chipped in all the same places and there were still holes large enough to put your fist in covering most of their walls. Everything was exactly the way it had been when I'd left. Nothing had changed apart from my view of the town. I'd wanted beauty and found filth, desired mutation and discovered stasis. The tape finished and clicked off, returning to the radio as I turned into the street I'd spent so much time in, so long ago. Elliot stirred. I reached over and shook him.

"Hey, you're home."

"Already? You made good time Flanagan, must have been doing ninety all the way," he said, stretching.

"About that," I nodded.

"You want to come in for a while? My folks would love to see you again," he added, gathering his shit together and unfastening his seat belt.

27

Did I want to go in? Revisit the only place I'd felt comfortable in as a kid, switch off and turn the clock back. His family hadn't cared who or what you were, they'd been content to just let you be. They'd had their rules, as all households did, but their rules were not the be all and end all. They were not carved into some book by which you had to live without deviation. His parents had encouraged me to express my opinions, to think for myself with no guidelines and no fixed menus. I could make my own selections and eat as much or as little as I liked. Elliot's Ma and Pa hadn't spent their waking hours at each other's throats, trying to score points in a no-win situation and his sister didn't torture you for amusement.

There was no collision between white collar supremacy and blue collar values; peace had reigned supreme. I didn't have to continually prove that I was worthy of their attention. Being there had been like living in a 1970's sitcom, 'Bless This House' or 'Happy Days', the fix that kept the real world at bay and I'd loved it. I could have trotted out a fucking tango in nothing but a pair of fluorescent socks and nobody would have said a word. His home had been a freakshow and I'd had a year round pass, reserved front row seats. The ones with the built-in headrests, when you settled into them, they wouldn't let you go. All I would have needed to complete the image was a bag of peanuts and I could have made merry with the clowns until the end of history. What kid didn't love the circus? I shook my head.

"Tell them I'll pop in before we leave. I've got to go check in at the hotel, see if I can get something to eat."

Elliot nodded, closed the door and walked down the driveway. I had to get going, get away as quickly as possible. If his parents had seen me, they would have invited me in and no wasn't an option that could even be considered. I could have argued, but they would have countered with their faultless, if somewhat bizarre, logic. I know that everything they did was done with feeling and although they never meant to, they always seemed to back me into a corner and with my back against the wall, all I could do was surrender. I imagined myself sitting at their table, their obligatory tea and cake hospitality being pumped into my bloating intestine.

"How are you Michael? And what have you been up to since we saw you last?"

They were the only people, apart from my mother who used my Christian name. I'd stopped using it and became Flanagan. Michael had died, he was a part of me that had been forgotten and left to decay. Michael had been an innocent who had savoured each moment, had held his breath as he digested the wonders of the world. Michael had been suffocated as Flanagan emerged, the infection that had spread through his body and taken over his being. Flanagan was all there was, a hate filled monstrosity that ate, slept and woke every morning with only one purpose. To consume each hour as it passed slowly over him. The alter ego had become the man and the man was nothing without the alter ego. What could I have told them? The truth?

"Oh, I'm fine. I feel like burning the entire fucking town to the ground and then blowing my brains out as the wind carries away the last of its ashes. Enough about me though. How are you?"

I pulled away and drove through the quiet streets, their correlation squeezing my soul, easing my fever and subduing my madness. I drove through instinct, wandering the halls of my old stomping ground. As the town dreamed, I thought of Papa Bear, the studio engineer who was mixing our record back in Boston, and what he'd said to me as we worked our way through a graveyard shift with Jack Daniel's and Marlboro.

"You guys can't lose. You package all this rebellion and hatred in a record and there are ten million teenagers out there ready to buy into anything that screams isolation and alienation.

"They know it's safe, because all you do is talk. It's all mouth and no action. Saying you hate the system and hoping it will go away is real cosy when you know you're going to sleep in a warm bed and eat the finest French cuisine.

"You punk rockers are all the same; playing something that caters for the kids who are going to end up running the world. You've taken something that used to be dangerous, tamed it, reinvented it, turned it into a soundtrack for suburbia and made a fortune from angst and depression. Man, I wish it had been this easy when I was one of those kids."

Driving through those streets his words made me realise what, at some level I'd always known. My life was a lie. Not a mistruth designed to divert and distract attention. It was a deliberate deception that had grown, unchecked, until it had burst through the confining glasshouse of the punk scene. There was no rags to riches story, no juvenile lashing out as his surroundings and making good. I was a well educated, middle class pretender who had played the rebel because he couldn't decide on a career. I'd never been fucked righteously morning, noon and night by big brother, never been trampled underfoot and forced to conform. I'd sat down and said no before I'd even been asked the question. I'd read a couple of chapters and made the ending up.

Deciding how the story was going to reach its climax without knowing all the facts. A spoilt little baby who howled when things didn't go his way or people tried to ignore him. A doppelganger who played it for laughs and the sympathy vote in a different shithole every night. The last thing you need when you're checking into a hotel is the self-doubt that comes with sharing what others have known right from the start; that you're full of shit. It's hard to maintain an image when the picture of yourself that you've painted has been scribbled on and desecrated by wax crayons. Instead of a battle weary veteran, all I could focus on was my day at the seaside with mummy and daddy. I parked in front of the hotel and gazed into the rear view mirror. Flanagan stared back at me and smiled as I started to sway in time with the hum of the engine. I had to pull it together. I rubbed my eyes, lit a cigarette and looked at the mirror again.

As I inhaled and exhaled, my reflection did the same, once, twice, three times. Concentration was paramount and knowing this I ground the cigarette out in the palm of my hand, twisting the filter until it was extinguished. Pain usually snaps you back to reality in an instant, but there are times, like when you've drifted a little too far, when it takes a split second for the nerve endings to react and carry the impulse. I watched my skin blister and smelled the savoury aroma of hot meat before I felt the pain. The tingling in my left hand grew, causing me to twitch as the impulses battered their way home. I curled my hands into fists and held on tight, relishing each moment of agony. Composed, I got out of the car, grabbed my bag and pushed my way through the revolving doors of the mortuary that served as a hotel. Its grey, imposing bulk rose up from the centre of the town, its shadows cloaking the 'family business' that huddled close for protection and security.

The lobby – or is it reception? Another of those international mysteries that scholars puzzle over as they hop from border to border trying to familiarise themselves with the bastardisation of communication and the corruption of language that separates and defines, was illuminated by fake Victorian street lamps which fed the eerie silence. Half expecting to have to claw my way through cobwebs, leaving a trail in the dust that had settled in the decades since anyone had stepped into the building, I walked over to the desk, put my bag on the floor and listened. Underneath the silence I could hear the faint laughter of shadows, trading small town tales. The reception barrier was jet black and drew the light that was cast out of the lamps toward it. I touched its frozen surface and snatched my hand back, as it screamed, shrieked and wailed, it's banshee cry making the message clear. Leave. I should have listened. Should have got back in the car and got the fuck away, never looking back. Good advice is hard to listen to when you're still getting used to the idea that bullshit pours through and from you like an ageing waterfall. I stroked and comforted my fear.

"Shh. It's alright; I'll call for a receptionist. Somebody's got to be here. Somewhere."

I tried peering around the corners, hoping that someone would deal with me before I disturbed the peace of the dead. My view was blocked from both sides. My pathetic bravery spoke for me.

"Hello?"

She appeared from the right and strolled briskly to the desk without looking up. "Yes?"

No eye contact. I stared at her, trying to imagine her daily life. About forty, brown hair, married to a man she barely spoke too. She'd spent too much time chasing divorced sailors in low rent bars and nightclubs. Alcohol and bitterness had taken their toll. Her best years had been wasted and were far behind her.

"I've got a reservation."

She looked up and did exactly what I expected her to do. Her smile disappeared as she studied me. It wasn't anything new. The staff at most of the places I've been booked into have treated me in the same manner. They judge by appearance and seeing a punk rocker, automatically think about the Sex Pistols and New Age Travellers. They convince themselves that there's no way on God's fertile earth that I can afford to pay the bill. Wankers. The first time it happened it did bother me, but I learned to live with it and make the most of their petty minded preconceptions. I invented a game that I've never grown tired of. It's called 'Guess The Sexual Preference'. I stared back at her and decided that contestant number one liked to be fucked in her arse. The harder the shunting, the more she'd cum. If she was left raw and bleeding, blood and semen running down her thighs, she was fulfilled. Ready to start again. I centred on a mental image of her, bent over a tattered sofa, held down by the brute she'd picked up that night, grimacing and crying as he forced himself inside her. Deeper and deeper.

"Yes sir, and what name is that reservation under?"

My breathing grew shallow and my heart rate increased as I became aroused by my own poisonous imagination. I leant against the desk in an effort to hide my growing erection. The banshee screamed and its talons ripped at the hole where my heart had once dwelt.

"Flanagan."

If I'd slapped her in the face she wouldn't have reacted differently.

"Oh God. I'm sorry Mr. Flanagan. We weren't expecting you yet. I'm so sorry."

She blushed, looked down and pretended to flick through the register. Her moans and soft whimpering filled my mind as I watched her turn page after page. Back and forth, back and forth. Had to hold on. Calm down.

"That's alright, happens to me all the time," I tried to laugh. All that would come was a nervous chuckle. Figured.

"If there's anything I can do," she began, staring at me, "anything at all, just let me know. I'm Elaine."

Fame can be a strange beast. Some doors it opens, some it slams shut, but once you've been bitten, your life will never be the same again. I'd never taken advantage of it, I'd been content to stay in the background and play out the straight man role that I'd been assigned by Elliot. But I needed this, needed something to hold on to. I swallowed.

"Anything?"

"Anything at all," she purred, smiling coyly.

I leaned forward, further and further, until my face brushed against hers and I whispered in her ear.

"I want to fuck you."

The wailing and moaning were converging. My head was aching. I felt nauseous. She giggled, kissed my cheek and softly returned my whisper.

"Anything for our guests."

I lifted the partition and let her lead me to a door marked 'office'. She opened it and I followed her inside, turned to face her and fell to my knees. I hitched her skirt up, tore her knickers away and placed my face between her legs, licking greedily at her sour nectar as she moaned and pushed down. I climbed to my feet, turned her around, held her skirt up and bent her over. Spreading her buttocks, I thrust forward, penetrating her rectum. She grunted and forced herself back, not wanting to miss an inch. I thrust, again and again...

"Mr. Flanagan, I'm so sorry. We weren't expecting you yet, I'm so sorry."
"What?"

She stared at me, puzzled.

"Are you alright Mr. Flanagan?"

I blinked, looked at her and closed my fist, putting pressure on the fresh burn.

"Sorry. I'm fine. I'm just tired; it's been a long day."

She smiled. "I understand. You're in room 35; I'll have someone take your bag up. Your guest is waiting in the dining room."

"Guest?"

"Yes, she arrived about an hour ago. Here's your key. If you need anything else someone will be on reception all night. Just pick up the telephone."

I nodded slowly, still in a daze. "Where's the dining room?"

Without looking up from the register, she pointed to a set of double doors to the left of the entrance.

"Straight through there sir. Enjoy your meal."

I thought my skull was going to explode and send tiny fragments of bone and gristle in every direction, redecorating the lobby, or whatever the fuck you call it, in a fetching shade of vermilion. I raised my hands to my head and pushed, trying to make sure that it held itself together. A thousand times, I'd played the game a thousand times, and never lost control. Power, it had always been about power, my way of developing a sense of power. Imagine the adversary at a base level and there was no danger of intimidation. I'd lost my grip and been sucked in, ground up and spat out. The certainty of who I was and what I was doing was dissolving and the solid credence that my destiny lay between A and B was clouding over. All I was sure of was that whatever faith I did have was gradually going the same way as the dinosaurs had.

I stumbled into the dining room, tapping the palm of my hand with my right index finger. Rows of empty tables filled the restaurant and I as adjusted to the subtlety of my new surroundings, the hypnotic repetition of the muzak that was piped in to add to the eating experience, eased my pain and solidified the liquid that coursed through my skull. She was sitting in the far corner of the room and as my sanity returned, I made my way towards her. Her brown hair hung loosely below her shoulders, smoke gliding above her. As I reached the table, she glanced up.

"Hello Flanagan."

Becky. Fuck, I should have known. It could only have been one of two women. After all, I didn't exactly have many friends in this town and my reputation as a Lothario was non-existent outside of my own imagination.

"Hello Becky."

I pulled a chair out, sat down and dragged myself to the table.

"You look disappointed Flanagan. Expecting someone else?"

As she spoke there was a flash of recognition that made me think of Alison and the performance art she had made a career from.

"No. I didn't think that anyone knew I was here. It's kind of a surprise that's all."

"Oh, and what kind of a surprise would that be?"

I took my jacket off and placed it on the back of the chair without taking my eyes off her and laughed.

"All surprises are special, but this one is especially nice."

Her cheeks flushed red; she reached for her cigarettes and offered me one. I accepted gratefully and took a light from her.

"I ordered you a beer, hope that's alright?" she asked tossing the lighter on to the table.

"Fine" I said, lifting the bottle to my mouth. It was warm and must have been left standing for some time.

"So, How are you?" Damn.

A question put forward through polite enquiry. Roll on the small talk. Surely we still had more to discuss than basic observation and the daily news? I ran my hand through the crew cut that had left precious little of my hair.

"Been better. How about you?" She sat back, smiled and shrugged.

"As good as you can be when all you do is write prescriptions and listen to the woes and problems of people you wouldn't normally give the time of day to."

She was a doctor? Jesus, I really was out of touch. I started to feel shitty about not trying to contact her. Not talking and sharing cases of export lager with her. I nodded.

"It's been too long Becky, I'm sorry. I should have made more of an effort to see you."

"You're here now and that's all that matters. I didn't think you were going to come back."

I traced the tattoo's that line my arms and spoke softly.

"School reunions, hell, there's an album's worth of material right there. What more does the international rock star need?"

She laughed.

"Is that what you are?"

I joined in, couldn't help myself. It felt good to laugh again. "No, but it's a living and it sure beats the shit out of working in a factory."

Becky stubbed her cigarette out, lit another and shook her head.

"These things are going to kill me. Seriously Flanagan, why haven't you been back?"

I pushed at the floor and tilted my chair back. A little more and the whole thing would have gone over and down would've gone Flanagan, beer and all; living on the edge and feeling the burn.

"I don't know. I guess I didn't think there was anything here worth coming back for." It was a stupid, arrogant response that only made her lash out at me.

"Really? What about your father's funeral Michael? That wasn't worth booking a ticket for, was it? What happened? Were you too busy playing to strangers and revelling in the sycophantic praise of arseholes to say goodbye?"

It's a well established fact that sarcasm is the chosen tool of the dimwit, but if it's used in just the right way it can reach between your legs and squeeze, hit you where you're most sensitive. I hadn't gone to his funeral, hadn't seen my father since I'd left the green grass of home in my wake. I hadn't liked the cheap prick when he was wasting Mother Nature's resources and sure as shit was brown, I wasn't going to play the dutiful son, weeping as I went through his portfolios, searching for the bargains he may have left. That's what the rest of my inbred family had been for and as far as I was concerned, they'd been welcome to the fucking lot. No, when I heard about him croaking, I broke out the champagne and went right back to watching television. Every worm in the cemetery had probably choked on his old bones as they tried to force him down. Just as unappetising in death as he had been in life.

"What the fuck would you know about it? He was one of the main fucking reasons I left." I hissed at her, dribbling beer.

I had to try to remember: swallow, then reply.

"Excuse me? Who's the doctor here? Who had to watch him waste away and die a little more every day? Who had to listen to him talking about you all the time? Michael this, Michael that. When is Michael coming? You have told Michael haven't you? The least you could have done was reply to the letters I sent. Sent a fucking card or some flowers to the funeral."

She couldn't hide her fury as she lectured me on family values and moral education. I knew it. If I started to feel good something was bound to come along and fuck it up. Rule eleven –'Feeling great? Remember it; because you'll end up paying for it tenfold'.

"I didn't read any of the letters. I never do if they carry a postmark from around here. I burn them. I can't face them. Can't look at them without thinking about what we did. Success and money can't buy release. I'm sorry, I couldn't come back...it wasn't...didn't feel right. Felt like I'd have been adding insult to injury, gloating. You know what I mean?"

I must have struck a nerve because she immediately backed down. "You still think about him as well Michael?"

"All the time. Sometimes he's all I think about. All I dream about. All I see."

She sighed, searching for imperfections in the moulding and construction of the table's surface.

"Yeah. I guess one of the advantages of being a doctor is self-diagnosis. If I can't sleep, I just pop a couple of pills and think about nothing. How do you deal with it?"

"Same way you do. Drugs and plenty of them. Shoot up and fade away, there are only pleasant dreams at the end of a needle. If I can't buy relief, I'll delay the problem as long as I can."

I thought she'd be shocked. Scream at me about HIV, hepatitis, septicaemia and all the other radical bullshit that scared parents and teachers worldwide. She only nodded.

"That why you had all the tattoo's done? Trying to hide the marks, keep the tracks a secret?"

"Nah, I'm in a punk band, remember? It's what I'm supposed to do. Get tattooed, swear at children, huff gas and abuse old ladies."

She started laughing again and coughed, gagging on her beer.

"Please don't make me laugh Michael. I'm trying to stay angry at you and that's hard enough as it is."

"Okay. No more laughing, no more fun. Serious topics only. Global warming, tree hugging, take your pick. Useless information is my speciality," I said, sitting bolt upright, stroking my chin.

"Will you fucking stop it?"

"Alright. I'll stop. One condition though."

"What's that?"

"Stop calling me Michael. That's what my mother calls me, and it makes me feel like I'm seven years old. It's Flanagan, just Flanagan."

"Very well Mr. Flanagan. Are we going to eat or sit here and get drunk?"

I shot her with my best withering stare, drained my beer, rolled my eyes skyward and answered.

"Madam, I was born ready."

We ordered, ate and avoided any conversation that might lead to the story teller. We swapped anecdotes, talked about her family and my family. I shattered a few illusions about life on the road and we moved onto the coffee. Manners cost nothing and I probably should have pointed this out to the waiter, but it was late and he was pissed off with having to stay and cater to our demands. I didn't think that he'd be open to any suggestions I might have concerning etiquette. Kept my mouth shut, just in case he decided to spit in the soup, wipe his dick on the main course and decorate the desert with the rat shit that can be found in any busy kitchen. After finishing the meal, we retreated to the bar and told the barman to keep the drinks coming and charge them to my room. The record company was paying and I thought that I might as well sting them for as much as I could. Perks of the job.

"Are you happy Flanagan?"

"Happy?"

"You know, are you happy doing what you do? Is it everything you thought it was going to be?"

Happy? It seemed strange that I hadn't thought about that before. I didn't even know if I'd experienced true happiness. Maybe I had in my own limited way. After all, I'd been up been down, been all around.

"No, it isn't like I thought it was going to be it's...I don't know. I write songs and I get to play them and see the world. As far as happiness goes... it's a job, better than most, worse than some. It's what I do."

"You haven't answered my question."

"Alright. Look, I've built a career on having a certain type of image and playing a certain type of music. I've built on a lie, added layer after layer of crap until I was left with the finished product, Flanagan. It's like a palace made out of shit. See it from a distance and you're dazzled by it, but the closer you get to it, the stronger the smell. Eventually, you get to touch it and when you do, it turns your stomach. What you see isn't always what you get."

She seemed horrified. "Doesn't that bother you?"

"That I'm living a lie? Not really. I mean there are aspects of it that do, like all the bullshit about crashing the establishment when I'm one of the few that take from the many. I guess the only thing that really bothers me is that while I was out there doing it, I forgot who I was. All there is now is Flanagan. Flanagan the media whore, Flanagan the punk rocker. The guy who's angry at the world and doesn't know why."

"You sound frightened."

"No, I'm not. I just wish I knew one way or another. If that is who I am, I'll have to learn to deal with it. If it isn't, how can I separate myself from him? He's all I know."

Becky shifted on her stool, reached out and touched my face. I wanted to recoil, slap her hand away. Instead, I placed my hand on top of hers and held it there.

"What happened to you Michael?"

Michael. I wanted to tell her that Michael was dead, that there was only Flanagan. My courage reared up on its hind legs, paused, tested the breeze, lowered itself, curled up and went back to sleep.

"I honestly wish I knew. Here I am, successful according to the literal definition of the word, my peers respect me or at least they pretend they do, and I can basically do whatever I like. But am I happy? I should be. I pushed and chased until I got what I wanted. Ironic isn't it? I've achieved exactly what I set out to and now that I've got it, I don't know if I want it anymore."

For the first time since I'd walked into the dining room, I saw her. Really saw her. She was beautiful. She leaned over, dressed in tight leather, consumed by passion.

"I'm yours Michael. Take me, fuck me, use your desire, and use it on me. Do what you want. Here, now."

I closed my eyes, counted back from one hundred, reached eighty-three, opened them again and spoke.

"Is medicine everything you thought it would be? Plenty of dashing surgeons to take your temperature and measure your heart rate?"

She pulled her hand away, fumbled for another cigarette, lit it and blew fresh smoke across the bar.

"You're joking aren't you? I'm nothing more than a shaman with a pill and a potion for every ache and pain. An amateur psychiatrist, who reassures the infirm and postpones the inevitable. Surgeons don't want doctors, they want bimbos who'll fuck them and look good at functions. Anything else is a threat to their fragile egos and I can do without having to support a God complex. The whole love and marriage thing seems to have passed me by, left me choking on its fumes."

"Whoa, slow down Becky. I'm the bitter one remember? Cynicism doesn't suit you. This is the nineties; you're supposed to be confident and self-assured."

That smile. I'll always remember Becky's smile. A perfect picture; frozen forever and flawless.

"What about you Michael? Have you ever been tempted to take the plunge? No model or actress caught your eye and made you want to settle down, vote to reduce taxes and own a Volvo?"

Every fucking day. Every time I thought about Alison, I wanted to stroll through the aisles of DIY superstores and open a charge account at Mothercare. Buy into the conservative dream, smoke a pipe, wear quilted slippers, bounce little Flanagans on my knee and tell them stories about giants and fairy princesses.

"If she's out there, I haven't met her yet. I don't exactly move in the circles where people discuss family values and mortgages. Coke habits, downers and deviancy don't qualify you for suburban life."

"I guess not. There must have been someone special, the one that got away?"

Alison, Alison, Alison. She'd never let me be free, we'd always be together, trapped in my mind.

"No, I've never been bitten and from what I've seen of every doomed attempt at love, I consider myself lucky."

I must have upset her. She seemed uncomfortable as she played with her cigarette.

"Maybe if you got laid a little more Michael, you wouldn't be so uptight. Relationships can work if you want them to, they don't always end in disaster."

Talk about plausible denial. A complete reversal in less time than it took to whip out your John Thomas and wave him at the neighbour's wife.

"Sound advice from the mistress of gloom. Shit, a minute ago you were all for mass castration, riding the feminist chariot to a female utopia. How about you, ever had that special guy?"

She signalled for another beer and looked at her feet. Bang. Slammed shut, locked out, denied. Fair's fair, shouldn't play the game if you don't want to compete.

"Come on, this is me you're talking to."

She lifted her beer, took a quick gulp and sighed.

"There was someone once. He didn't feel the same way about me and I never bothered telling him."

"Ah, shit Becky, I'm sorry. You must have loved him a lot."

Welcome home Flanagan, the perfidious martyr who eased his guilt with spurious recantations and trivial apologies. She smiled.

"More than he will ever know. I still do. He was in love with someone else and I didn't want to be with him if he was always thinking about her. I didn't want to be the third party in my own love life."

I understood. I'd been the third party for as long as I could remember. Watching, as a cast of thousands tasted the fruit I never would. Watching and waiting alone in the dark.

"Hey Becky, I didn't mean to upset you. Let's just forget it, okay?"

"Same old Michael. Same tired old routine. Don't patronise me, I might start to think that you actually care."

Falling into bad habits. Self-obsession and ignorance are malicious bedfellows. Man, at that moment I felt really fucking small.

"Of course I care."

Surprising how easy that one came out. Liar, liar, pants on fire. The flames tickled my balls and I blushed, suddenly aware of the scabs I'd been picking at.

"Whatever you say," she sighed. "A little late, but it's still nice to hear you say it."

Stay calm, water off a duck's back, hold the reigns and paddle like fuck. Cool wet grass, making angels in the cool wet grass. Change the subject, flip the disc and run for the border.

"So, you know what anyone else is up to these days?" I enquired as casually as I could. Under the circumstances I think I did a fucking good job.

"Nice touch Michael," she replied, grinning. "What do you call that? Damage limitation?"

I wasn't about to rise to the challenge and struggled to shrug her comments off while I tried to remove the imaginary dagger she'd thrust into my chest.

"If you don't know, just say so. I'm not going to be offended."

"I didn't say that Michael. Some of us care about our so-called friends."

She was right. I knew it and she knew it. Maybe she could have cushioned the blow, but when you've got a point to make you might as well hammer it home instead of dancing around the side lines.

"I'm sorry okay? I know I've been a motherfucker, but I'm trying. I'm full of shit and my apologies and explanations can't make up for whatever it is I've done, but I am trying. So come on, give me a chance. Please?"

I thought I saw a tear forming in the corner of her eye; she brushed it away, smiled wearily and nodded.

"No, I'm sorry. I don't mean to take this out on you. I'm just so fucking angry and tired. You got out and got on with your life and I feel like I was left behind propping the gates open in case you decided to visit."

I leaned forward, held her hands and kissed her forehead. I wondered what it would be like to be inside her, feeling her breasts tremble as she reached climax. Not that she would with me.

"It's alright, I'm not going anywhere, and I'm here now. If I'd known how you felt..."

"What would you have done? Dropped everything and run home? Come on Michael, it wouldn't have made any difference. You're only taking this shit because you're here. It's not like I didn't have the opportunity to leave. I stayed. End of story, okay?"

"Okay."

I smiled, gave her a hug, wished I hadn't as my crotch came alive, sat down and reached for a beer. Would I have dropped whatever I was doing and come back if she'd asked me to? Thinking about it only swelled the self-loathing that I already felt. There was nothing that could have dragged me back, persuaded me to drop anchor in this one horse burb. If you have to think about doing something for too long, then it's probably a bad idea. Probably. My groin throbbed as the pressure shot toward the red and I winced, startling Becky. She broke free of my embrace and stared at me.

"What's wrong Michael?"

I had to think fast. Be nonchalant and not let my fear of my own desire reject her.

"Nothing I'm fine."

"Really? Then what just happened?"

Facing the truth isn't the same as accepting it. There's always another option. You can take a peek, ignore what doesn't suit you and hope it goes away or you can take it to heart, learn from it and grow. Then, while you're growing maybe you can move into a tepee, plant some fucking lentils and give peace a chance with the rest of the retro flower children. Neither appealed to me, so I settled for a happy medium. I took a pinch of fact, blended it with a sprinkling of fantasy and spoon fed it to Becky as required.

"There's nothing wrong. I'm not used to being this close to women. It throws me off balance. It takes some getting used to."

She frowned, considered my answer and spoke quietly.

"Please don't lie to me Michael. I know all about the seedy underbelly that goes hand in hand with what you do."

The look she gave me defined the meaning of hurt and brought it right into focus.

"Becky, I swear I'm telling the truth. I haven't been this close to a woman for a long time."

I'd said more than I meant to, but I'd managed to keep my raging hard-on a secret. That was something I didn't think she'd appreciate me sharing with her.

"Come on Michael, yank it harder and bells might ring." She said the words, but didn't believe them. I heard the doubt in her voice.

"No really." I said firmly. "But what you do..."

"Because I play music for a living, I've got to be a whore right? Got to take part in that circus, go with the flow and take advantage of everything on offer?" I said flatly.

"Well yes..." she stammered, embarrassed by her assumption.

"It's not like that. I sit on a bus for twenty hours a day, get off when it's time to play and get back on when I'm finished. When I'm not on tour I keep myself to myself. Write songs, watch television and get ready to do it all again." I spoke slowly and clearly, making sure she understood what it was I was telling her.

"If you don't, you know, live that life, why do you do it?" she asked.

"Because for two hours I can forget about everything. I can lose myself in it lose myself in Flanagan. It's a powerful drug, being up there doing it. Once you've tasted it, you can't get enough."

I felt her hand rest itself on my knee, felt her nails as they dragged across the fabric of my jeans. I tried to think about anything that would distract me, keep me from concentrating on her touch.

"Don't you get lonely Michael?"

I thought about tax returns, the cubic capacity of a 1969 Chevrolet Camaro, the Cyrillic alphabet and the genetic predisposition of the offspring of alcoholics; anything that would serve as a distraction. If she'd squeezed, I wouldn't have been able to do anything except smoke a cigarette, roll over and go to sleep.

"I'm used to it. I don't think about it anymore."

"I can't believe that anyone who has the world at their fingertips would choose to live like that," she said incredulously. "I mean you can have anything you want and you just let it all slide past. I can't believe it."

"Believe it." I said curtly. "Anyway, we're getting away from the point. Stop trying to avoid my question. Do you, or don't you know what anyone else is up to?"

"Okay Michael, you win."

She brightened up and became the girl I used to know. The one I remembered, who sat patiently and listened while I serenaded her with songs of death and destruction. The one person who wasn't afraid to tell me that I was repeating the same chords, ripping off someone else's idea or dwelling on my favourite teenage subject, Satan, a little too much. She seemed happier knowing that my life wasn't a bed of roses and that I dwelt in a hell that I'd been instrumental in creating. It's always a blessing when you learn that misery loves nothing as much as she loves company. It's a relief knowing that you're not alone. The seconds slipped achingly away, hanging in space before they fell into infinity and were pursued by their brothers and sisters, who followed in the footsteps of their kin, savouring the spotlight before they tumbled away.

"Well?"

My patience was being stretched to its limits and ironed flat.

"Sorry," she apologised, shocked back to reality "I was a million miles away. Where do you want me to start?"

"Where ever you want," I said, waving my hand wearily.

It's not that I wasn't interested; this was the easiest way to maintain the conversation without it becoming complicated. Without having to reveal any more of the things that I'd become so adept at hiding. Besides, it looked like she was going to dine out for a month on what I'd already given her.

"I suppose you know about Alison?"

"Uh huh, I still read the papers y' know."

What had Elliot called her? A skank? Where the fuck had he pulled that one from? Another part of his tough guy act. A small fish trying to hand out beat downs in the big pond.

"Funny isn't it? You're famous for being a bad guy who made good, and she's notorious for being the good girl who likes to be bad."

"Notorious? You sure that's the right word?" I asked quietly.

"What else would you call her? She fucks guys on film, Michael. I think that's a pretty fair judgement."

"So, the world's oldest profession has moved into the video age. Voyeurism is the safest sex anyone can have. What's the big deal?"

"The big deal Michael is that this is a small town and most of the people here are still trying to come to terms with the free love epidemic of the sixties and when a local councillor's daughter puts the town on every map for all the wrong reasons there's bound to be trouble. I watched her family as they tried to understand why she turned her back on them. Jesus Christ Michael, I can't see how you can be so calm about it."

"What she does isn't any of my business. Get over it. I did."

"Just like that?"

"Uh huh."

"This isn't some soap opera we're talking about Michael. She's..."

I interrupted her. I had to keep this particular closet shut. Weld the airtight seal and hold the vacuum.

"I know what we're talking about but there's nothing I can do to change it or her. It's none of my business what she does."

"It must be nice to have a liberal attitude and live in an anything goes world Michael. Unfortunately, I'm not in that position. I can't sit back and let life pass me by. It's demeaning, watching her perform, selling herself like a piece of meat."

"Does it affect your life? Nobody said you had to watch."

"Maybe it doesn't affect the way I live, but that doesn't mean that I don't think about it. It doesn't change the way I feel. Just because I can't watch her it doesn't mean that I've stopped caring about her or the way she's perceived."

"Right, okay, but if she doesn't care, why should you? All that should matter to you is how people see you. It's all about choices. She made hers, I made mine and you made yours. It doesn't bother you that I do it."

I should have let it go, shouldn't have dragged myself into the equation. Should have let it slide, put all the pieces in a box and folded it neatly away.

"It's hardly the same fucking thing Michael."

"Of course it is."

She leaned towards me, making sure that she could detect every twitch, every tick and that nothing would escape her attention.

"Okay Michael, explain it to me."

"You really need me to explain? Fine. We both play roles that Joe Public believes because, hey, if you see it, it's got to be true right? That's all there is to this person or that one, the image they present. So, all that you are, everything that makes you who you are, is a doctor. Nothing more. All that's really being sold is time. Whether it's your time, Alison's time or my time. We're all pieces of meat available for consumption. It's all a game."

"That's it, is it? The universe according to Michael Flanagan. Ladies and gentlemen, Flanagan knows the secret to the meaning of life. You want to know what it is? Life's a game."

"We're not talking about life."

"Oh really? Then what are we talking about Michael?"

"Entertainment."

"Entertainment? Hell, why don't we bring on the jugglers and a family of acrobats? Shit, you could take the show out with you and hold matinee performances. You'd pack them in, have them rolling in the aisles."

"Becky, just because you don't like something, it doesn't mean that someone else won't. Variety is the spice of life. If there's one lesson I've had to learn the hard way, it's that even if something makes your skin crawl, you've got to live and let live. Fuck, it's the only way you're going to get through any of this shit."

Dispirited, she placed her drink on the bar and spoke again. Her voice was heavy with disappointment.

"I just didn't think that you would enjoy that kind of thing Michael. Thinking that you do, seems... I don't know..."

"I didn't say that I enjoyed it. All I said was that it was her choice and it wasn't any of my business. If you wanted to know how I felt about what she does, you should have asked."

"Well, how do you feel about...How can I put this...? Alison's career?"

Her question made me smile. Funny, I hadn't felt like smiling. I was probably better at repressing emotion than I'd realised. Choose one and do the opposite, holding the original in reserve. Hey coach, you going to give me a chance to get in the game? Sorry kid, it isn't the right time. You'll get your opportunity don't worry. Relax and enjoy the festivities. It's beer and skittles from here on in.

"What do you want me to tell you? That it rips my heart out knowing that she felt she had to do it? Knowing that anyone feels they need to do it? I guess she isn't the person she was. I hate it and try to avoid thinking about it. The girl I knew wouldn't have done it, but if you fall for cold hard cash, it's going to rub off on you. You can't fall in love with it and not become a little like it. It's a cruel world and Alison is an example of its avarice and corruption."

Silence. We'd fallen into one of those awkward moments that I associate with chess tournaments. Neither of us wanted to break free of its possessive restraint. Didn't want to test the ice in case it wasn't solid, wasn't uniform in its density. Becky skated out first.

"Taylor's a policeman. Well, he's drug squad, plain clothes, doing all the exciting stuff."

I shuddered. It felt like someone had walked over my grave. Then turned around, retraced their footsteps, stopped, unzipped their flies and pissed on my headstone.

"Busting kids for smoking weed huh? Oh, I can barely contain myself. I'm just swelling with pride knowing that he's part of that thin blue line that prevents society from collapsing into lawlessness. Doesn't it make you feel good knowing that he's out there watching over you?"

She giggled. A schoolgirl laugh. The kind that drifted toward you when you were trying to catch a glimpse of tit through the crack in the roof of their changing rooms.

"So you're still their biggest fan then Michael?"

"Sure, I'm the poster boy for their recruitment campaigns. I've even got a uniform hanging in my wardrobe. I don't know what's worse. The fact that he's a pig or that he's drug squad."

"Who's judging the book by its cover now?"

"Maybe, but it just seems like history is repeating itself. It's the hippie thing all over again."

"Michael, you've lost me. I haven't got a clue what you're talking about" she laughed.

"Selling out," I replied softly. "Its fine to kick out against the system when you're young, then suddenly your priorities blur and instead of trying to change what's wrong, you welcome it with open arms. Jump aboard the slow ride to power and riches. You become a hypocrite without realising it's happening and end up being part of the do as I say not as I do collective that shapes the rules and regulations to suit themselves. We're all destined to become our parents in the end. The more things change, the more they stay the same."

"Stop being so fucking morbid. So, he joined the police, forget it. It doesn't mean that he's responsible for all the shitty things that happen."

"No, but if you're not part of the solution, you're part of the problem." I lit a cigarette, tasting the sweet Virginia smoke as it filled my mouth.

"I can't figure you out Michael. One minute you're telling me that you hate playing the role of punk rock supremo and the next you're waving the revolutionary banner and sloganeering. Talking about smashing the State. Just who the hell are you?"

"A part time urban guerrilla whose social conscience won't let him lead an average life. It's in the blood."

"Maybe it's time for you to grow up and join the real world."

"Don't. You sound like my mother," I said, groaning.

"Someone has to, you bad, bad boy," she cackled, wagging a finger at me. Feigning injury, I hung my head and mumbled

"It's not fair; you're always picking on me."

I laughed and put my hand on her knee. She glanced down at it, blushed and smiled. I brought my outburst under control before speaking again.

"Taylor's a fascist, what about Blake?"

"Oh, he's around and about," she said dismissively.

"I don't want to know where he is; I want to know what he's doing. He's probably running some corporation that flattens everything in its path knowing him."

"Michael."

She paused, looked away, sighed and started again. "After you left, Blake, he, uh, had a few problems."

"Problems?"

"It's probably just as well that you hear it from me. He had a breakdown and had to leave college. He's been here ever since."

Feeling like an arsehole was becoming a regular occurrence. I had to try and pry my feet out of my mouth without making it to obvious.

"Fuck. I didn't know."

"Don't start apologising again Michael. What's done is done."

"Is he, you know, weird and shit?" I asked carefully.

"He doesn't dribble and rant about Jesus if that's what you mean," she frowned. "He seems happy enough working in the video store. A little intense at times, but that's nothing new."

"As long as he doesn't turn up covered in war paint, quoting from the Book of Revelations and waving an Uzi around, I think I'll be able to cope," I joked.

"You never know," she laughed nervously.

"Becky you'd better be taking the piss or I'll have to change my underwear and pack a bullet proof vest."

"No, he's fine honestly. The vest was a nice idea though."

"What happened to him?"

"Who knows? Guilt, sorrow, getting too wrapped up in those strange films of his. Could be any one or all of a million things. Some people just snap."

"Yeah. You see it on the box all the time, but you never think it'll happen to you or someone you know."

"Why not? It happens all the time. Could have been you, could have been me. It's not selective. It was Blake's time, that's all."

I was starting to become uncomfortable with the idea. The thought of the threads of my mind snapping, one by one, bounced around and I had to cut its momentum. Stop it before it became contagious.

"So, you got a hot date lined up for tomorrow night?"

"No. I thought I'd turn up, check out the action and if I can get drunk enough, pick up the nearest poor bastard and fuck his brains out. I've got needs you know Michael," she said flatly.

It shocked me, hearing her talk like that. I decided to go with the flow, if I didn't ask now, I'd never get around to it. I'd keep finding excuses to put it off. The sky's blue, it's a Friday. Wouldn't have mattered what it was, I'd have used it. One thing I was good at was procrastinating. I wasn't just good at it, I was a fucking master.

"I thought that maybe we could go together. Not like a date or anything because it always looks better if you don't turn up alone. You don't seem so desperate...I mean, you don't have to fuck me you can find someone when you get there, because it's not a date and we're not a couple... I just thought that maybe the company would be nice."

"I'd like that Michael."

I almost missed her reply, too busy tying myself up in knots to think straight.

"You would?" I stammered.

"Yes. Don't sound so surprised. You never know, you might get lucky," she said coyly.

Shock is a violent experience, steamrollering you, blanking your mind, frying your senses, making speech an impossibility. She must have thought I was having a cardiac episode.

"Errrgh..."

"Michael, I'm joking. Relax, I'm joking."

Having a panic attack, sitting in the middle of the bar reminded why it was that I didn't get laid as often as I would have liked. Sex had become like Christmas, coming around once a year, leaving only disappointment in its aftermath. I could do this; I was doing this. I just had to try and remember how to do it.

"Uh, so how do you want to play it? Meet there, me pick you up, what?" I squeaked between shallow breaths.

"How about you pick me up at eight? That way we'll get there before the entertainment kicks in and there should still be enough booze left to get nicely toasted."

"Oh yeah, cranked to the eyeballs and picking fights. I'll drink to that." I said, raising my bottle.

"If you're going to make a fool of yourself, I'll pretend I don't know you," she replied sternly. "I'll behave, I promise."

"You'd better Michael or I'll beat the shit out of you."

"Hey, you can trust me."

"Uh huh. A million white bread kids can't be wrong, so I'll go with popular opinion and give you the benefit of the doubt. Just this once though, don't go getting any ideas of grandeur," she continued, and she finished her drink.

"What else have you got planned for tomorrow?"

"You know, stuff. Thought I'd take a wander, see how things have changed." "That should fill about an hour. Want to meet up?"

I thought about her suggestion. I really did. For about two seconds. My mother used to tell me to never put something off until tomorrow if it could be done today; whatever that meant. Fucking great time to start taking parental advice, but it was all about timing. The past was catching up with me and there was no point clinging to the life vest when the rescue choppers picked you up.

"Nah, there's some shit I've got to take care of. If I keep putting it off I'll never do it."

Becky smiled, that fucking smile that made me want to wrap her in cling film and play pimps and hookers, and then she looked at her watch.

"On that note Michael, I'll leave you to it. I've got to try and grab some sleep while it's still dark."

"Sleep my dear, is for the weak."

"Don't," she laughed. "I want to look like I'm at least half alive tomorrow." "Fuck it, join the undead. Talking about tomorrow, where do I pick you up?"

"Same place. I know it's pathetic, a twenty eight year old still living with her parents, but the rent's cheap and the food's good."

"Don't I know it. I'll see you tomorrow then?"

She leaned over, kissed my cheek and whispered, "You bet. It's good to have you home Michael."

As she stood up, she straightened her skirt in a fluid movement that all women learn when they're young, turned and walked to the dining room entrance. I watched her, watched her arse as she strode confidently away. I tried to picture her as the girl I'd known, but the two images couldn't agree with each other and squared up, ready to go in their individual corners. Plain Becky had become Doctor Lust, the PhD you'd demand a hernia check from. Being a late bloomer must have had some benefits, I couldn't think of a single one and gave up trying to identify them before I overheated. I finished my drink, one thought keeping my smile in place. I had a date, which was something of a minor miracle. Now all I needed was the sugar that turned itself into angel dust on command and I'd be set. I squeezed my sack again and felt the nausea. Becky reached the door, looked back and blew me a kiss. Pretending to catch the kiss was difficult. My stomach was telling my mouth to open wide and prepare for evacuation. My arms were numb, but there was too much resting on returning the gesture. Catching thin air, clutching at it, hurt. It was worth it though. To feel alive and not take the whole shebang for granted like I usually did. To savour it, absorb it and utilise it. I waved as she left and steadied myself, pain and alcohol seriously fucking with my sense of balance, and made my way toward the elevator in reception.

Having watched too many 70s disaster epics, I've always had an irrational fear of metal boxes that rise and fall at the touch of a button. Who knows what can happen? Electrical failure, the gears seizing, the cable fraying, there are any number of misfortunes waiting to trap you, screaming for help, slowly wasting oxygen. Asphyxiation can't be a pleasant way to go, clawing for one last lung full. If it could happen to Lorne Greene, what hope did I have? I looked at the elevator, told myself I was being stupid and took the stairs. The nice, safe, firm stairs.

5:08 A.M. August 29th, 1998

Success is bankable, and the room I'd been given reflected what the hotel manager imagined my material value to be. Under direct pressure from his superiors no doubt. Everybody has to answer to somebody. Four poster beds, Jacuzzis and complimentary champagne might help to set the mood for stressed out executives on their way to a thrombosis, but they've always intimidated me and emphasised the fact that I feel like a fraud. Comfort is a luxury that you soon learn to live without when you spend three quarters of your life dashing from city to city. Too much like greasing your pole with the sweat of the oppressed subjects of hierarchical censorship. I flicked the light switch on and smiled. The staff had taken the stories they'd heard about petulant rock stars seriously and bolted the television in place. Clamped and secured it, just in case I got a little carried away. Making a mental note to smash it into firewood with one of the emergency axes that were dotted throughout the building in convenient locations, I spotted my bag that had been dumped on the bed. It would be a shame to leave without giving the staff something to talk about, seeing how they'd gone to such great lengths to make me feel welcome. I looked at the clock on the bureau below the window. It was far too late to crash out and much too early to do anything of consequence.

Unzipping my bag, I checked to make sure that the head of PR had behaved and done as I'd asked. Hidden under a pair of faded jeans was the skag I'd pleaded with her to slip in my luggage after we'd passed through customs. All the headlines that rant about how such and such was caught smuggling or trying to acquire dope are bullshit. When you're famous you employ people to do it for you. If they get busted, there's no comeback and you can wash your hands of a messy situation. No one gives a fuck if Mr. or Mrs. Normality get caught with a condom of Pakistan's finest stuck up his or her arse, if they know your face though, there's too many questions that have to be answered. I've seen it too many times to believe that there's any discretion in the judicial system. Scandal sells and there's enough profit to spread around, enough for everyone to cop an equal share. You'll only get caught if you're either stupid or want to, and if you want to be caught, then you deserve everything you get. Don't give me any of that crap about the inner child screaming for assistance. Dumb motherfuckers are the only people who want to sit in press conferences confessing their shame and asking for forgiveness. Stupidity gets you an enforced stay at Betty Ford or five to ten with Billy Ray Jim Bob and his favourite tube of lube.

Laying the neatly tied bag on the bed, I searched through my luggage until I found what I needed. A couple of loose syringes that had been bundled in as an afterthought, my trusty leather belt, lemon juice and the one item I never left home without. Ritual, every user has a ritual; a certain way of doing things that is as much a part of the habit as the drug itself. Mess with your ritual and the jitters kick in, reducing the effect. If you don't follow your pattern to the letter, you might as well flush the dope; it isn't going to do you any good. I removed the blanket that I'd kept with me since that night at the cliffs, felt its smooth familiarity, folded it and placed it on the bed next to the dope. Junkies are some of the most organised people I know. You've got to be when your only reason for living stops you feeling like a turd that's been squashed in the gutter. Getting organised becomes easier with time. You get used to it, switch off and do it without even thinking. Each item gets laid out in accordance with individual preference. I've always gone with juice, needle, spoon – taken

from the tea set that the hotel staff had kindly left, and then smack. I've got to admit, as I established the order, I started laughing. Picturing the rep running around Soho trying to score was pretty amusing; she got to act out all her criminal fantasies and maybe she realised that being bad always felt good. I hoped that was how she'd seen it. The alternative was pitiful. A blubbering mess permanently looking over her shoulder wasn't an image that filled me with joy. It made me realise that I was playing at being a rock star, which made the role I'd assumed of pretender, far more realistic. I shook my head. Fuck reality, I needed to escape. I measured the powder on to the spoon and added a few drops of lemon juice. Apparently, it's all down to the acidity helping to balance the alkaline composition of heroin. Chemistry wasn't a subject I'd been enamoured by and the only pharmaceuticals I was ever interested in were sold on street corners. I dropped a filter that I'd torn from a cigarette into the mixture and heated it. As soon as it began to bubble, I sucked the fluid into the syringe, placed the needle on the blanket and left it to cool.

Popping a vein isn't as hard as some documentaries make it out to be. Sure, if you're habitual, there's the danger of overusing a vein and collapsing it. The secret lies in using different ones as often as you can. Again, where you shoot your dope is part of the ritual and seeing as my usage was kind of conventional, I've always gone for the arms. They're easier to tie off, raising their veins. I once met a guy who used to shoot into his neck but that struck me as kind of excessive and the tried, trusted, traditional methods worked just as well for me. Arranging a chair in front of the window so that I'd have a sea view, I tightened my belt into a tourniquet, sat down and pushed the needle in. The question of purity never even crossed my mind. Strength didn't matter as long as the heroin hit my brain like an inbound freight train. Shit, even if I'd got a hot shot that would have been just fine with me. Over, finished, gone, done, out, without any hysteria. Pushing the plunger is part of the thrill, almost a lucky dip, you don't know what you're going to get and for a brief moment you're aware of the boundary that stands between control and pleasure. Watching your blood enter the barrel and then re-enter your body is surreal, almost sexual. As consciousness melted, I slumped in the chair and watched the sunrise, dawn's light pouring through the window over my inert body.

Playwrights and romance novelists will try to convince you that dawn is a time for lovers, to be savoured engaged in congress. Personally, I think that you'll never truly experience its magnificence unless you're shot through with the contents of a half-gram wrap. Never feel its warmth, never see the way its ray's gradually creep across your limbs, never touch the centre of its naked display and never understand its rarity or beauty. A beauty that gets brushed away in the rush of busy commuters too preoccupied to pause and see what's right in front of them. Taken for granted and ignored, the little things that matter fade away, growing dimmer and dimmer, winking out of existence, missed by nobody.

As the sunlight filtered through the net curtains and crept sluggishly along the carpeted floor, I drifted in and out and dreamt of the storyteller banished to limbo with only my father for company. Both of them trapped in the shadowy cosmos, inhabiting a plain that flourished on the guilt and sorrow of the material world. The cabalistic odd couple clinging to my shoulders, their claws forever embedded in my spine. I'd grown tired of the burden, grown tired of nourishing them, grown tired of their whispering and plotting. Release through inebriation was my only recourse and even then they chased me down, tightening their hold. When their weight had become too much, as it often had, I'd stood on a stool with a noose around my neck, daring myself to take that crucial step. Uncertainty always crept in at the last minute to remind me that the odds were uneven. Damnation or salvation. Until I was sure which path I'd take, the rope would hang empty from the rafters. I tried to stay under as long as I could, the opiate clouding my perception, blocking the subliminal messages and the pervasive chatter that spoke of paradise and invited punishment and ordered convergence.

Normality slowly seeped back in, my blood thinned and the mixture dissipated. Rising toward a crescendo, the babbling was kept in time by a thumping that echoed over and over again; a click track that kept a constant rhythm. I heard the scrape of metal as a key turned in the lock. Scrambling to my feet, I leapt at the door, knocking the chair over in the process. I thought I'd go through it, hitting it full force, the wood splintering as I struck it. It held, the handle rattled and I groped for it, my panic desperately trying to silence it. I forced my shoulder into the door in an effort to prevent its gloss finish from leaving the frame and shouted as pleasantly as I could.

"Yes, who is it?"

The reply was barely audible above the throbbing that danced from my left temple to my right and back again.

"Housekeeping, sir."

Housekeeping. It flooded back. Hotel. I was in a hotel, where jobs that needed be done and guests had to be kept happy. My pulse raced, the belt slid from my arm as it fumbled against the door and I surveyed the room. There on the bed, right where I'd left it was the bag of magic carpet ride and the carbon scoured spoon. I had, as some doomed general had once said, 'A plan A and a plan B'. Plan A would have involved apology, explanation, the police and an octogenarian judge. A banjo played the theme to 'Deliverance' and I voted for plan B. Indignation. I was going to bluff my way out.

"Could you come back later? I've only just woken up; I haven't even had a shower yet." The voice that rested against the other side of the door paused and then answered. "Sorry to have disturbed you sir. I'll come back later."

I stayed where I was for a full five minutes, not quite believing that the maid had left. For all I knew she was still there, waiting for me to move before bursting in and catching me red handed, which would have been more embarrassing than being outsmarted by Scooby Doo and those interfering rich brats that he hung around with. What the fuck would I have said?

"I would have got away with it, if it hadn't been for that pesky cleaning lady."

It didn't quite have the same ring to it, didn't sound as convincing as the cartoon villains. After thinking about Shaggy, Fred, the Mystery Machine and the other two, I still can't remember their names, and trying to work out how they actually made enough money to keep their van running, I walked over to the bed and packed the potential crisis back into my luggage, keeping one eye fixed on the door. Trust funds. Had to be trust funds; that was the only way they could have gone nationwide, playing detectives without jobs. Satisfied that I'd folded the bag and spoon into the blanket and returned them to their proper place, I headed to the bathroom and climbed into the shower, thought about it for a moment, decided against the idea and started to run a bath. My head was pounding, it felt like a hangover was kicking in and if it feels and looks like a hangover, you can be fucking sure it is a hangover. I checked the mirror.

A pale, shallow complexion and bloodshot eyes stared back at me and confirmed what I already knew. That I'd hopped aboard the last train to hangover city. To be absolutely certain, I poked my tongue out and saw what appeared to be fuzzy, furry shit lining it. I pulled it back in before hypochondria took over and convinced me that I'd contracted the Ebola virus. Alcohol and drugs are supposed to be a musician's best friends, but I had an unusually low tolerance for both. I loved them and they hated me. I'd managed to get over the stage of puking every time I shot up and could drink all night as long as I didn't mix the grape and the grain, but it had taken a lot of practice. Straightening out and being hungover at the same time doesn't exactly keep you sharp and on your toes and ready to immediately spring into action. I pushed my fingers down my throat to see if there was anything that needed to come up, gagged and spat, did it again, gagged and tried to spit. There wasn't enough liquid in my mouth to coat my tongue. Seeing the bath was half full, I turned the taps off and jumped in. And, drowning in fear and dread, I thought about the evening that lay ahead.

10:09 A.M. August 29th, 1998

School reunions serve no purpose other than to recreate the melodramas that most former pupils thought they'd left behind. They're never like they are in the movies, where the victims have all turned their lives around and the in-crowd have all fallen flat on their arses. No sir that just doesn't happen in the real world. Popularity and success don't diminish. If you start out as a winner, then you're going to finish triumphant. Good genetics build confidence and make anything possible. If you can dream about it, you can be it. Perfection makes school a breeze. Friends, parties, a non-stop social event punctuated by the kind of academic prosperity that creates proud parents. A slight flaw in the genetic code and you're fucked for life. The only thing you'll be taught in the classroom is how to fail and once you're assigned that particular role, you learn to live it so well that it soon becomes second nature. It becomes a brand you'll wear until your dying day, a marker that singles you out so that everyone can recognise you for what you really are; a loser. It's the foul smell that follows you from job to job, keeps you down and prevents you from rising above your station. It kills hope faster than Zyklon B. These reunions are never organised by the bullied or the weak, they're the property of the beautiful people. Their way of reminding any of the unlucky souls who may have been fortunate enough to forget old times that they still lord it over whomever the fuck they want to. Of course, the invitation can always be ignored, but they never are. Why? Because there's always a remote possibility that time has healed the scars and you'll be welcomed as a long lost brother or sister. Just like there's a chance that all of the armies of the world are going to lay their weapons down and play patty cake with each other. It's a nice thought, but that's all it is.

Lying in the bath, I thought about the days I'd spent being indoctrinated in the hellish institution that was sometimes referred to as a beacon of learning. Too weird for the in-crowd and too strange for the rest of the population, I'd been left on periphery, an observer recording the behaviour of his fellow prisoners. I'd taken the beatings, but as I spent my evenings at shows, slam dancing for fun, they hadn't been a big deal. The perpetrators soon grew tired and became demoralised as I laughed off their best efforts at conditioning. They marked me down as a lost cause. After that it was smooth sailing, they did their thing and I did mine, counting down the days until it all ended and we could all get the fuck out of there.

The steam hit the cold surface of the mirror and began to condense and I thought about my invitation. Initially, I'd screwed it up and thrown it out and went right back to laying my guitar tracks down. Elliot had other ideas though and got straight on the phone to the one of label's publicists who nearly creamed himself. He raved about what a great angle it would make, how we could tie it in with the release of the new record. Guys, you can't buy publicity like that had been his favourite line and he tried beating me into submission with it. Reluctant agreement is part and parcel of the business.

They suggest, you refuse, they demand and you walk out. Then you reach a compromise. Objective achieved. I'd asked Elliot why he was so adamant about attending and his only response had been an incoherent mumble, something about 'showing the fuckers'. After a while, I'd given up and fallen in line, pretending to roll with it like I usually did.

To Elliot, it was all about leaders and followers, cowboys and Indians. He was Big Chief Talkshit and I was the humble brave ready to die on command. The possibility that I might have my own reasons for coming back and that I'd just played hard to get hadn't occurred to him until we were well on our way home. Even then it had barely troubled him, a passing fancy that was easily eliminated and laid to rest with a brief question. The only person I was there for was me. Fuck Elliot and fuck the label, this time it was personal. I stretched my legs out and pulled the plug, letting the water drain away, watching as it obeyed Coriolis' Law, the whirlpool increasing in diameter as the water's volume decreased. I struggled out of the bath and briskly dried myself off with a towel. I still felt like shit and thought that I'd be more at home lying on a slab in a coroner's office. It was time to face the world though and face it with a smile. I stared into the mirror, beckoned my reflection to come a little closer and spoke gently.

"Today's the day. Remember, you're a bad motherfucker. Attitude and balls are the only things that matter, and no fucker is going to stand in your way. It's time to finish it."

I winked, saluted myself, turned about and walked back into the bedroom, over to my bag and pulled out the first shirt and pair of jeans that came to hand. Black on black, Johnny Cash would have been proud of me. Humming 'Folsom Prison Blues' I removed the blanket, folded it carefully put my dope and lifeline paraphernalia back into the bag underneath a Bad Religion tour shirt that had become a dirty grey colour following repeated washes. Yeah, that's right, even punks use soap powder. I slipped my ensemble on and hunted for the car keys. I shook the pants that I'd been wearing the previous evening, heard the familiar jingle of loose change and keys and breathed a sigh of relief. Hot wiring the car with a screwdriver would have required a degree of concentration that just wasn't going to be possible, not to mention a vague understanding of what you're doing. Picking the blanket up, I took a last cursory look around before leaving and decided to throw my bag into the bottom of the wardrobe. I locked the closet, took the key and put it in my pocket. None of the hotel staff were going to supplement their wages with anything that belonged to me, and I didn't want to return to find a blue rinse victim of an overdose lying in a pool of her own vomit. Content that I'd covered all the bases, I stepped into the corridor, slammed the door and headed for reception. Daylight alters things, changing them in the blink of an eye. Reception wasn't the vault of terrors that it had been when I'd arrived. It had a friendly, casual atmosphere; its dark corners drew the light in and opened up, increasing the foyer's size. I made my way towards the revolving doors that separated me from my mission.

"Mr. Flanagan?"

The voice had come from behind and I turned to face whoever it was that was trying to grab my attention. She was young, early to mid-twenties and pretty. Not in a conventional sense, more in the girl next door kind of way. Management must have decided to play the Jekyll and Hyde card with the hotel. Keep it smart and presentable during business hours and wheel out the ugly truth after nightfall. Equal opportunity was the cruellest joke that the government had ever implemented. Another set of rules whose very word and every letter could be twisted and manipulated this way and that and still remain within the law.

"Yes?"

Realising that she had my undivided interest made her blush and she looked away, refusing to maintain eye contact. I hate that. If you've got something to say, say it to my face, I'm not going to bite your head off. Not unless I'm really hungry.

"Your suit arrived this morning sir. What do you want me to do with it?"

Clever responses and witty repartee are the bread and butter of the acting profession. Unfortunately, I've never been quick enough to bang them out on the spot or knock them off the then and there production line. They always seem to float in after I've replayed the conversation a dozen or so times.

Given a bit of leeway I could probably have come up with something along the lines of "Well, you could put it on, lap dance to 'Holiday in Cambodia' and let me stuff notes up your hoohah, if you're so inclined."

However, all I could manage was "Thank you. Could you have it taken up to my room please? It's number 35."

Whatever she'd expected me to do or say, it sure as hell wasn't the same as the reply she'd been given. Maybe she thought I'd start foaming at the mouth, screeching about the Seven Plains of Hell while slashing at myself with a rusted cutthroat razor. Flick the switch and there I was, the one and only unholy Flanagan. Her luck was out. It wasn't midnight, I wasn't sitting on a pumpkin and my fairy godmother was a strung out hooker working the corner down from Mann's Chinese Theatre on Sunset Boulevard.

"Of course sir. Uh, I was wondering, that is, if it isn't too much trouble, if I could have your autograph? It's for my brother; he's a big fan of yours."

Uh uh, no way, fuck you, cram your superfluous request up your arse. It had been so long since I'd been asked that I barely remembered how to react. Pick up a pen, sign your name and make cheap comments about the weather. Saying I was stunned would have been like swallowing ground glass; painfully stupid.

"Yeah, sure," I began "who do I make it out to? What's his name?"

She reached under the counter and produced a stack of compact discs that she placed next to the register.

"It's Stephen. I hope you don't mind, but when he heard you were staying here, he nagged me to ask you. Sorry."

Any hope of privacy that I might have had, had just flown out of the window. I waved it goodbye as it sped away.

"That's okay; it's nice to be asked." I laughed.

She nodded but her mannerism told me that she didn't believe a word I'd said. I laid the grisly blanket on the counter, complied with her request and handed her the key to my room. After I finished, I picked the blanket up again and walked back to the revolving door, pushing against it as I entered its confining entrance. The sunlight blinded me and I blinked to try and remove the permits of the coloured dots that had created their themed discotheque in my retinas. I opened the car's boot, threw the blanket in and walked around to the driver's side. Stopping to take note of the surrounding town, I inhaled deeply, tasting the air. Nothing. Its putrid odour was gone, replaced by the salt that hangs in the air, stiff and unmoving, in all coastal towns. It's supposedly adds character and ambience, that is, it does if you believe the sugar coated crap that tourist boards feed visitors to make sure that they don't run screaming for the nearest available exit. I unlocked the door and climbed behind the wheel, pulled out of the car park, and on to the main road. It took me a while to get used to driving on the left and as soon as I thought I'd made the adjustment, a tiny voice came from out of nowhere, some far distant point of my mind, criticising and needling me. It sounded exactly like my dad used to when I wasn't doing something the way he would have.

"Are you sure this is right? It doesn't feel right to me. Are you sure you're doing it correctly? Whoops, mirror, signal, manoeuvre. Not too fast, foot covering the brake. Don't you listen to anything I say?"

Holding the wheel in place, I searched through the glove compartment, trying to find a tape I could play that would drown out the voice in my head and help me ignore its persistent whine. My fingers wrapped themselves around a cassette box; I pulled it out, flipped it open and slid it into the stereo. I was greeted by a Californian accent shouting about the forthcoming war and how I'd better be prepared to kiss my balls goodbye in a mushroom cloud that rained atomic debris. Oh yeah, I was ready, willing and able to do that. I just needed a moment to figure out how to deal with the deal with the very real problem of that pesky extra vertebra. Twisting the volume as high as it would go, I laughed to myself. That would shut the fucker up. He'd hated punk rock. Couldn't understand a word they were singing, if you could call that singing he'd told me whenever I'd put a record on. If you want to listen to music, listen to music and not that noise.

My dad always had far too much to say for himself, especially when it came to things he knew nothing about. He was a walking encyclopaedia filled with blank pages who had built a bridge that neither of us wanted to cross. I stayed on my side and he wouldn't move from his. By the time I left there was nothing left to say. He didn't want to listen to me and I'd heard more than enough of who he thought I should be. I turned the air conditioning on and headed for the beach, oblivious to anything outside the car, concentrating on the doctrinal poetry that was pumping through the speakers.

I pulled onto the common that acted as a car park, left the engine running and leaned on the steering wheel. It was the same old story. Eleven forty-three and there were barely any spaces. Give people a few hours of sunshine and they'll swarm to the beach, paddle in the ocean and make sandcastles until they drop. The great British summer brought all the human insects out until the sun disappeared over the horizon's yardarm. I left the stereo playing and watched fat children in skin tight shorts and bikini's waddle toward the waiting sand, their even fatter parents shouting at them in between mouthfuls of ice cream. Closing my eyes, I focused on the sound that filtered through my steel cage. I let my memory take over, miming the words as they reached me.

"Wait, will you bloody wait."

"Just you wait until I get my hands on you. Then you'll be sorry."

"No you can't have a hot dog."

"Your father's busy, can't you see that?"

"Well, I don't know where you left it, do I?"

"It's got to be in here. I remember packing it."

"If you don't start behaving, we'll get right back in the car and go home."
"Frank slow down, I can't walk as fast as you."

"If you go running off, you'll get lost and that'll be that."

It was the same old story. A new generation of adventurers but their tales were all the same. And they came flooding back so easily; it was almost as if I hadn't been away. Ten years wiped away in a dream. A dream of family vendetta's and organised trips that was stuck in an endless loop, treading the same path over and over until it was worn away. And when that trail finally disappeared, they'd just repave it, add another layer of tarmac and start again. I switched the engine off, got out of the car and followed them, listening as they wished their lives away. They were too fat to run and too stupid to hide and I listened intently as they pulled each other in and began to drown.

12:23 P.M. August 29th, 1998

Every step was an effort, a battle that raged, as the opposing armies of light and darkness fought for control of my soul I forged onward, resolution and fatigue the only allies that rallied to my cause. Helped by their iron will, I struggled against the midday sun as my flesh cooked and sweat boiled, dragging my cross through the soft sand, inch by inch. Shackled underneath its weight, my legs buckled, I stumbled, regaining my footing by anchoring myself against the illusory trench that the crucifix cut. The ghosts of the travellers who had assembled on the desert plain slipped from the future, through to the present and into the past, their chatter mocking me as I continued my pilgrimage. How long I baked in the sun was irrelevant, all that mattered was that I reached the cave, reached its shelter. Once there I could melt into the darkness, cast off my burden and retreat to lick my wounds. Inside the cave was the treasure I had left behind so many years ago, the peace and freedom that I had exchanged for complicity that had been handed over with no thought of consequence, swapped for a chance to rummage through the bargain basement that Elliot had swung open and laid bare. I was ready to demand my deposit back and return the bills of goods I'd been sold without warning. But I had to prepare, I had to show piety, I had to repent and prostrate myself on the road to salvation.

As I reached the cliff base, butterflies fluttered through the aviary in my stomach. Instinct took over as I started to ascend, finding all the handholds and ledges that I remembered from a lifetime before. Something inside me wanted them to have been washed away, eroded by the elements, hoped they'd disappeared and that I'd be denied the release I sought. Nature is the only constant, civilisations may rise and fall, species may flourish and decay, but nature remains, its laws unspoilt and unbroken. My fingers bled and my muscles ached, life and tobacco had taken their toll and sheer determination was the only thing that bound me to the face of the cold granite. I pulled myself over the final obstacle and lay there listening to the air rattle through my chest. Crawling to the edge, I stared out over the wasteland and began my descent, carefully traversing the gaps between the ledges and outcrops. Sensing the support of the rocks below, I jumped backwards into space. Before me, the mouth of the cave stretched itself into a toothless grin and I stood, waiting at its entrance. Breathing deeply, I closed my eyes and crossed its threshold.

"Hello Flanagan."

I slowly opened one eye, stopping its lid at a narrow crack and traced the direction of the sound. Crouched at the back of the cave was a silhouette that had merged with the shadows. Hidden from the entrance, it was lit solely by the thin slivers of light that dived through the maw of the cavity. Moving closer, I peeked at it, hoping for recognition. The grey streaks in his hair and the paunch that hung over his belt made him look older than he was.

"Taylor?"

"I've been waiting for you to show up Flanagan. Punctual and predictable as ever," he said, holding out his hand for me to shake. "How are you?"

Gripping his hand, I pulled him into a bear hug. Letting go was hard. For all my bullshit about betrayal and selling out, I'd missed him. Missed talking to him, missed being around him, missed the jokes he used to tell. The ones that never went anywhere, never had a punch line and always left me feeling slightly confused. I let go and had a closer look at him in the limited, available light. If pressure made you age before your time, here was a man who had taken up the slack and immersed himself in his nightmares.

"Better for seeing you," I nodded. "How did you know I'd come here?"

"It's my job to know what the criminal elements are up to, second guess them and catch them in the act," he answered sternly.

"Alright, you got me. It's a fair cop, but society is to blame. One thing officer, how did you catch me?" I asked in a feeble attempt at a Cockney accent. It sounded more South African, but a dialect is a dialect, regional pride aside.

"Ah well sir, you broke the golden rule of getting away with it. Never return to the scene of the crime without establishing a concrete alibi first."

"I'm not saying anything. Get me a lawyer and then I'll spill the beans."

Taylor doubled over laughing and waved me away. I smiled. He looked like he needed to laugh. He straightened up and brushed himself off, chuckling.

"It's good to see you Michael. It's been too long."

I sighed. "Wish I could say the same. You look like shit Carl. What happened?"

He rubbed his eyes. "Life Michael, life happened. I got a real job, got married, had a kid, got divorced, started drinking and didn't swan off around the world getting my dick sucked in every town. It all mounts up."

"What the fuck is it with you people? You all think I'm living the life of fucking Reilly, strutting around like some bloody prima donna with a legion of flunkeys to wipe my arse and stroke my ego," I spat, trying to get the cigarettes out of my pocket.

"Sorry Michael. It's hard not to think like that when you read all those stories in the music magazines. It's difficult to see the person you used to be."

"Look, you don't want to believe all that shit. They make half of it up to sell a few extra copies of their crappy rags."

"And the other half?" he grinned.

"Well, you've got to have some fun," I replied, returning his grin.

"Yeah, I'll bet you do. So come on, tell me some stories about the rich and shameless."

"Well," I began, "we all have cocaine blown up our arseholes by tiny servants that we buy from a corner store in New York. They import them from Africa."

"You're shitting me?" he gasped.

I stared at him. Being in the police force had turned his brain into mush. It wasn't just a rumour. The law really did have a machine that lowered your IQ.

"Of course I am, you fucking lunatic. They really get them from Australia."

"Fuck you Flanagan."

"Yeah, and the horse I rode in on too."

"Oh yeah. First you fuck them, then you eat them."

I laughed and finally managed to free the cigarettes from the recesses of my jeans. The packet was bent and crumpled, but its contents were still intact. I offered him one and he shook his head.

"No thanks. I quit a couple of years ago."

"Suit yourself. I thought all pigs lived on a diet of coffee, nicotine and doughnuts."

"Coffee and doughnuts are the property of the US police. Over here, its whiskey and all day fry ups at greasy spoons. It's a sponsorship thing. They don't fuck with our deal and we don't mess with theirs."

"Right, I forgot. It must be the jet lag, crossing all those time zones."

Nodding, he reached into his pocket, pulled out a hip flask and took a swig. He offered it to me, I declined. Looking the way he did, I didn't even want to think about what was swirling around inside it. Turpentine or floor polish maybe. Whatever it was, it had probably put hairs on his chest, his palms and the soles of his feet.

Taylor drank and I smoked. We tried to find some neutrality, a way of re-establishing our bond, a back door to slip in through and a way of easing ourselves towards the inevitable.

"You bumped into anyone else yet?"

I felt the smoke trickling down my throat and savoured the flavour. No doubt about it, I was well on my way to Marlboro country.

"Yeah, I saw Becky last night. We had dinner and played catch up." Taylor smiled and kicked feebly at the uneven floor of the cave.

"I might have known that she'd be there to welcome you back," he muttered. "First in line to congratulate the conquering hero."

I flicked my butt against the rocks; the glowing filter rebounded and dismissed a brigade of fiery ash as it struck its target.

"What do you mean, 'I might have known she'd be there'?" I stared at the ash as its embers surrendered and became cold.

"It doesn't matter."

Damn evasive police procedure. Dangling the carrot in front of me and then snatching it away when I tried to take a bite. Casting off and reeling me in.

"What doesn't matter?"

"You really don't know, do you?"

This interview session bullshit pissed me off. I was supposed to be his friend, not some toe rag he'd pulled in to fit up and throw down the stairs when he wasn't satisfied by the indirect arguments the scumbag used as a defence.

"Really don't know what?" I pleaded.

Did he want me to go down on my hands and knees and beg?

"Michael, if you don't know about Becky by now, you never will. If you can't figure it out, ask me again later."

He wasn't about to tell me and I wasn't going to flatter him by allowing him to hold whatever it was he knew over me. Barking at his ankles like a puppy eager for attention from his master. Michael Flanagan kissed no fucker's arse. Not even for all the coke in Bolivia. I let it hang there, on the end of his tongue. If he didn't spit it out, he was going to have to swallow it.

"She told me about Blake."

"Yeah? Told you about him going spastic did she? Told you about him attacking that girl and getting sent to the nuthouse did she?"

I buried my horror and barely flinched at the revelation. At last some small town scandal that didn't involve midnight rendezvous or the illicit use of bondage equipment in front room torture chambers. Something that didn't involve Alison, Elliot or me. Fresh meat for the grinder.

"She, uh... she didn't go into detail. What happened?"

He produced the flask again, unscrewed the top and paused.

"Seems that our friend Blake watched one too many of his videos and thought he'd try to be Ed Gein. He cut some poor girl up pretty good, left her some nice scars to remember him by. When they caught him, he wouldn't shut up. Didn't just confess, he actually seemed proud of what he'd done. His lawyer entered a plea of insanity; the judge accepted it and he spent two years reflecting on his crime with the boys in white. Gulping down Thorazine and watching television. They should have thrown away the key and kept him there."

"Say hello to the caring, sharing police force of the 90s," I replied sarcastically.

"You're fucking right. We're the only ones who do care," he snapped. "I see that sick fucker all the time, watch him check in with all the other perverts, kiddie freaks and rapists. Signs his name, smiles and goes back to his life. I've looked into his eyes, seen him for what he really is. It's still in there. He liked it and he's going to do it again."

"Everyone deserves a second chance Carl," I said quietly.

"Not that fucker. Someone should bundle him into a car, drive him out to some deserted lane and cut his head off. Do us all a favour."

"Someone like you Carl?"

"Why not?" he spat. "Better than leaving him to do it again, letting him mutilate someone else's daughter. Next time he'll get it right and there won't be any counselling or plastic surgery, just a corpse that's been carved up like a Christmas turkey."

I watched the directionless rage surge through him, twist him and eat him. Watched the veins on the side of his neck throb and pulsate. I understood why he'd aged. Understood, but couldn't sympathise. He'd taken on the sins of the world and been crippled by their unforgiving demands.

"This isn't about Blake is it Carl? It's about you. How you deal with it. How you live with the memory, day in, day out, without being able to do anything about it."

"I don't know what you're talking about."

His jaw was trembling and he couldn't meet my gaze.

"Hello? I was there too Carl, remember? We threw him over the cliff and watched him float away. You think it doesn't bother me? It keeps me awake at night. Every fucking time I close my eyes I see him, hear his voice, it's all

I think about."

He leapt at me, wrapped his hands around my throat and slammed me into the rock face. His eyes shone with raw, undiluted fury.

"That's exactly what I think Michael," he roared. "I think it doesn't fucking bother you at all. If it did you wouldn't have run off with your faggot friend, leaving the rest of us to try and make some fucking sense out of the whole bloody mess. You nailed it in one Michael. Hooray for you, the boy done well. How about a round of applause for Ma Flanagan's favourite son? The rock star came home to tell us how we should feel."

Motherfucker was a lot stronger than I remembered and I wriggled to try and break free. Every time I moved, he pushed harder. I was choking and in desperation, kicked out, my foot striking him in the groin. The pressure eased and he fell to his knees, clutching at the space between his legs. Coughing and gasping, the rocks supported me as I laboured against unconsciousness. I aimed a punch at his jaw, drew my arm back and let fire with all the energy I could muster. My fist connected with his skull, he grunted and collapsed on his left side. Waves of agony rocketed up my right arm. It felt like I'd been sparring with an anvil. Like striking iron with a matchstick. Boxers made it look so easy. Fifteen rounds of that shit would have killed me. Next time I'd hit him somewhere soft. Like the flabby envelope that hung over the waist-band of his pants. Circling him, I shook my hand in an effort to try and restore some feeling.

"Fuck you Taylor," I whispered "Fuck you. I didn't ask you to stay. I didn't stop you leaving, didn't stand in your way or hold you back. It's not my fault. If you want to blame someone, blame yourself you fat piece of shit. I didn't run after anyone, I went because I wanted to. None of you thought twice about sticking around for me, you all left me behind, remember? The only difference between you and me is that you came back and I stayed gone."

Taylor sat up and wiped the trickle of blood that was seeping from the corner of his mouth with the back of his hand.

"Why did you come back Michael?"

Disappearing into yourself and expressing your anger is fine as long as you stay focused on what's going on around you. Just because you're internalising your fury, it doesn't mean that everyone else is going to do the same.

"What?"

"Why did you come back Michael? Why now?"

I stopped, my hand hung in the air and I stared at him.

"I was sent an invitation for the reunion and I thought that it might be nice to come home and see some old friends. Guess I was wrong about that wasn't I?"

"That's it, is it? That's all there is to it?"

"Yeah."

"You're full of shit Michael. If you only came back for the reunion, what are you doing here? Why come here?"

I sighed, sat next to him, reached for a cigarette, lit it and smiled. "I don't know. Maybe to see if anything had changed, or what would happen if I came here. I don't know why. If you're looking for answers, I haven't got any. I don't know why I came here; it just seemed like the right thing to do."

"The right thing to do?"

"Am I under arrest?"

"No, though I should charge you with assault. That's hell of a punch you've got there."

I laughed.

"Fucking hurt me more than you by the looks of things. Alright, it seemed right, to come here and wait a while. Maybe try to apologise, make amends. I don't know."

"You can't change the past Michael," he said sadly. "God knows I've tried. Tried to dedicate myself to change by doing something to make up for what happened."

"That why you joined the police?"

"Probably. I thought I could keep the shit off the streets and make the world a little safer. But that's all turned to shit now."

"What do you mean?"

"Give me one of those fucking things will you?" he said, pointing to my cigarettes.

"I thought you'd given up?"

"Yeah, well I just started again," he muttered, cupping his hands to his mouth as I lit the cigarette

"Christ. I'd forgotten how good these things tasted. I might as well die happy. Enjoy it while I can, right Michael?"

"You don't have to convince me. What do you mean it's all turned to shit?"

"This is where it all started, where everything went wrong. You ever think about what might have happened if we hadn't come here that night? If we hadn't helped Elliot? How your life might be different if it wasn't for that one fucking mistake? How it might have turned out?"

"All the time Carl, all the time. Carl, what's turned to shit?"

Sucking methodically at the filter, he glanced at me.

"They've re-opened the case. Decided to have another look at it, examine all the facts to make sure they got it right the first time."

"Carl, if this is your idea of a joke, then it isn't very fucking funny."

He smiled. It wasn't a trick of the shade he did look old. Too old. The bags under his eyes and the crow's feet added an unwanted melancholic wisdom.

"It's no joke. After all this time, it's been re-opened and reassigned."

"Why?" I croaked, fear constricted my throat and squeezed my larynx. "Politics, my boy, politics," he answered miserably.

Fear. That was what I could smell. Fear riding the breeze and filling my mind. I wanted to run, get away, and get the fuck out of Dodge. Immerse myself in work and forget that I'd ever been here.

"Politics?"

"Yeah, politics. Apparently when you kill someone it's prudent to check that they're not related to anyone important. People the rules don't apply to. The sort of people who say jump and the chief constable asks how high."

"Important?"

"Oh yeah, our guy was well connected. He used to be the head of a business empire, right up until he dropped a little too much cash into the market. Things went belly up and he cracked, split in fucking two and then vanished into thin air. That is, he did until we came along."

"Connected?"

"Don't go losing the plot on me Michael. Are you listening?"

I nodded slowly and felt the calcium in my bones turn to rubber and jelly as fear pounded them with lead filled facts.

"The body was about to go in the ground as a John Doe, when these suits turned up, claimed it and started going through the case with a fine tooth comb. They made all these big city noises about sloppy police work, demanded an independent autopsy, all kinds of shit. This is a small town and nobody wanted to waste money on what they thought was an open and shut case. Wino has too much, slips on the rocks, falls in the drink, drowns and gets battered to shit on the rocks, then washed up on the beach. As far as the locals were concerned, that was all there was to it."

"If it was that simple why bother re-opening it?"

"Stop interrupting me and I'll tell you. Neither side wanted to budge. The coroner eventually recorded a verdict of accidental death. They buried him up at Saint Luke's, underneath this marble monstrosity, all the executives cried their crocodile tears and that was that…"

"Saint Luke's? Isn't that the one on the way out of town?"

"Jesus, Michael. Yes, that's the one. You can't miss it, big iron gates and old stone walls. Are you going to let me finish?"

"Yeah. Sure. Sorry."

I gazed at the ocean through the entrance. On a clear day you could see for miles and miles.

"Right, where was I? Okay, so they planted him and that's how it stayed until last year. The lawyers and the board kept everything ticking over until his daughter was interested enough to take over the mantle and wear the crown. Soon as she did, the bad times started rolling and the shit hit the fan."

Most of what Taylor said flew straight over my head as I sat, staring out at the ocean, searching for far off distant lands. He continued.

"First thing she does is announce the construction of a couple of new factories and this area was one of the locations that were considered in the feasibility study. So they applied for planning permission and with unemployment topping the national average, there wasn't a fucking hope in hell that it would be refused. Every councillor and department officer was delighted with the prospect of having their wheels greased and living on easy street. Then the board begins stalling and the council held an emergency meeting with them to see if the project could be salvaged. This went on for weeks behind closed doors. Finally the company announces a massive investment, one that would help to rebuild and revitalise the area, and the order comes down from on high to reopen the case, exhume the body and look for anything that might have been missed."

"So, the company held the council by the balls until they agreed to all of its terms?"

"Who knows what goes on when those doors close and the lights go out in the corridors of power? I'm just telling you what I know."

"You're in with the boys in blue, have they got enough to take the case seriously?"

"When a body full of formaldehyde has been in the ground as long as he had, it's pretty difficult to gather physical evidence. Anything conclusive anyway. Forensics ran their tests and the pathologist examined the body. The results were all the same. Inconclusive."

"So they're sticking with the original verdict, letting it go?"

"I didn't say that Michael. The tests were inconclusive. Not enough evidence to prove what actually happened, not enough to support the findings of the original coroner and not enough to prove any wrong doing. The case stays open. It's an ongoing investigation."

"Carl, it's a small town, you said so yourself. You must know the investigating officer or whatever it is you pricks call him. Can't you find out what's going on, how the case is developing?"

"You pricks?"

"Sorry. It was a slip of the tongue."

"Don't worry about it. I've been called far worse. Besides, I've read the files we've got on you. Kind of funny I thought, the tough guy crying like a baby every time he was brought in. Oh no, it wasn't me officer, I don't know anything. I was at home all night, you can phone my mother, she'll tell you."

If I sounded anything like his shrill, falsetto impersonation I really was in fucking trouble; up to my eyeballs in it.

"Ha, ha, you've had a good laugh, I'm glad you thought it was funny. So, do you know the guy or don't you?"

"You could say that."

"Carl, it's a simple question. Do you or don't you know the pig, ah, I mean, officer in charge?"

"Yes Michael, I do know him."

"Will he talk to you about it, let you know what's going on?"

"Oh, he'll talk about it all right. Sometimes it's all he talks about."

"You know him pretty well then huh? Back slapping buddies, funny handshakes and knees bent, knees bent ra, ra, ra. What's he told you?"

"Nothing I didn't know already."

"Stop playing fucking games and tell me Carl."

He squinted at me, his pale eyes moist with tears. "It's me Michael; I'm the one they've given it to. Me."

"Fuck me."

What could I have said? What could I have done? Patted him on the head and told him that everything was going to be okay? That shit happens for a reason and what goes around, comes around? Somehow I didn't think that the notion of karma would have made him feel any better and wouldn't have helped him to pick up the pieces and carry on. It hadn't done me any good, the idea of spirituality and the 'judge not less you be judged' arrangement that people put so much faith in.

"Ironic isn't it? Out of a squad of ten officers, the file lands on my desk and falls right into my lap, the only person who could definitively solve the riddle. I'm telling you Mikey, God's got a sick sense of humour. Investigating myself, it'd be funny if it wasn't so fucking pathetic."

So this was cosmic intervention. This was what it felt like to be touched by the hand of God, the Supreme Being, the universe, whatever it was that was in control of our lives. Strange, it felt more like a stroke to me. I had to remember to tell the medical profession. You know when a blood vessel ruptures in your brain and you end up bent out of shape? That's nothing to do with cholesterol or stress. It's Jehovah poking his finger into your grey matter, twisting it around, taking a scoop and serving it as a dip at one of his dinner parties. Check the data; I think you'll be pleasantly surprised. If I could just stop the bleeding and regain control of my left side, everything might just work itself out.

"What are you going to do?"

"Hmmm? What can I do? Same rules still apply. If I turn any of you in, I'll be turning myself in. Do you know what they do to coppers in gaol? I'm going to keep the case open. It's safer for everyone."

"Can you do that?"

"No problem at all. The only person who cares about it is the boss and he just wants it to go away. He doesn't like bureaucrats telling him how to do his job, especially if they're on the take. It's the pyramid thing. The buck keeps getting passed down until someone grabs it by the horns and wrestles it to the ground. I may not be able to fit into a leotard, but I can still fight."

"You can't keep going like this Carl. You're bound to make a mistake and when you do, we're all screwed."

"Why not? As long as I go to see the boss, keep him updated and juggle a few facts around, why can't I? It'll go away eventually. People lose interest in things. The minute my overtime gets cancelled, the file disappears and things go back to normal."

"Just like it did the first time huh Carl?"

"No, this time it stays gone. It's about appearances and making people happy. Long as it looks like I'm doing something, she's happy. The suits are happy because the money keeps flowing and my boss is happy because he's not taking shit from upstairs. She's happy, they're happy, we're all fucking happy."

"Happy to lock it away, hush it up and hope that one day you'll be able to live with yourself. Is that it Carl?"

"Michael, I've done a lot of shitty things since I started this job and I live with myself just fine. I'm not going to let one stupid mistake I made as a kid ruin everything I've worked for. I've got too much to lose. I want to see my daughter grow up; I don't want her visiting her father in prison. There's no fucking way I'm going to let that happen. Believe me Michael you've got nothing to worry about. There aren't going to be any arrests, it'll all blow over and be forgotten."

"I don't think I'll ever forget and I'm damn sure his daughter won't."

"No neither will I, but I can make it go away and stop it fucking with me. How about you Michael, can you live with it, can you cope?"

Honesty, he wanted honesty. And what the policeman wants, the policeman gets.

"No Carl, I can't. I've let it fuck me and slowly kill me for ten years and there's no way I'm leaving town without trying to do something about it."

"Before you get on your high horse and deliver a sermon from your soap box Michael, let me give you a bit of friendly advice. Confession isn't good for the soul. Gaol isn't a holiday camp; the inmates will be waiting in line to get their hands on you. Shit, they'll probably go for you before they go for me and I'm the one who's responsible for half of them being there. Think about it before you do it okay? Think really hard."

That was the problem, I was thinking about it. That was all I was doing. Thinking about what I was going to do. Throw myself to the lions and plead for leniency? Ten years after the fact the only thing they'd give me was life without the possibility of parole. I stared at Carl and imagined him taking his daughter to amusement parks and attending parent-teacher evenings. Listening intently as each subject master showered her with praise and congratulated him on the superb job he was doing, raising such a wonderful child in this day and age. It couldn't be easy they'd tell him and he'd agree. But it was a fuck of a lot easier to imagine Carl in that situation, than it was having to think about his daughter asking her mother why daddy wasn't there for her birthday. And it was a lot less painful too. My conscience had launched a sneak attack and if my emotions were going to demonstrate their bellicosity, I wanted to be on the winning team and there to share in the spoils of victory.

"How old is she Carl? Your daughter?"

"Sara will be four next January. Why?"

"When you see her, thank her. She just saved all our arses from the gaol house."

"You're not going to the police, Michael?"

"There's no point. Turning us all in won't bring him back and going to prison won't make up for what we did. It'll only fuck more lives up and I'm tired of always being blamed for someone else's misery. No, I'm not going to the police Carl."

"Thank you Michael. Thank you."

"Just out of curiosity Carl. What would you have done if I'd have said I was going to turn myself in?"

"I'd have stopped you."

"How?"

"You really don't want to know that."

He was right. I didn't want to know. I could imagine what he would have done, what he was capable of and that was enough for me. More than enough.

"Are you sure it's going to go away for good this time?"

"By the time I'm finished with it, no one will ever go looking for him again."

"I've got your word on that have I Carl? I've got your word that no one will ever knock on my door and ask me to accompany them to the station to answer a few questions?"

"I promise you that will never happen Michael."

"Then that's all I need. There's just one thing that's still bothering me."

"What's that?"

"When I saw Becky last night, she told me that you were Drug Squad and yet here you are in charge of what could be a murder investigation."

"Yeah and..."

"I'm wondering why someone who usually turns over dealers and busts pushers would be given a case like this. It doesn't make sense"

"If you're looking for sense and order Michael, the modern police force is the last place you're going to find it. I joined on one of those fast track programmes, the ones where they rush you through the ranks if you show promise, and part of the deal is that you get shunted from department to department. Most of the time I don't know what I'll be doing when I turn up for work. It keeps life interesting."

"Yeah, I'll bet it does. You never know whose head you're going to crack do you?"

"Fucking right. One minute I could be taking a payoff from a protection racket and a couple of hours later be getting head from a whore who can't afford to spend a night in the cells and miss out on the action she gets from her regular clients."

"I knew it. You pigs are more interested in what you can make on the streets than doing the job you're paid to do."

"Got you."

Taylor grinned, and then started rocking with laughter. "Yeah, you got me. Really had me going you prick."

At least he'd developed a sense of humour that he could share with other people. If the police hadn't done anything else for him, they'd prepared him for a moonlight career as a stand-up comedian. Telling mother in law jokes on the end of the promenade in some northern fishing town that had dried up and died in the aftermath of the Second World War.

"Carl, you said earlier that if I couldn't figure it out, you'd tell me what was so funny about Becky turning up last night."

"Yeah, I remember."

He was still laughing and obviously impressed with his newly discovered jocular prowess.

"Are you going to tell me, or do I just sit here and watch your tits jiggle? Didn't you ever think about a training bra or getting some exercise? They look fucking disgusting."

"I get all the exercise I need raising a glass from a bar to my mouth. What's wrong with my tits? Don't you like breasts? Prefer firm, hard young men do you Flanagan? Don't you like the ladies?"

"I'm easy sweetie."

I blew him a kiss and wiggled my tongue at him.

"Now that is fucking disgusting. Put that thing away before I cut it off."
"Whatever you say darling. It's your dime, not mine. You're the boss."

"Fuck, I've missed you Michael."

"Don't go getting any strange ideas, like the feeling might be mutual. I, unlike you, have many acquaintances, chums, pals and friends that I can rely on to be discreet in times of trouble."

"Always the comedian huh, Mikey? I think you missed your true vocation."
"Funny I was going to say the same thing about you. Come on, tell me

about Becky."

"You really are a witless bastard aren't you? Think about it. She's there waiting for you to arrive at the hotel and stays for dinner. Did she stay the night as well?"

"No she fucking didn't, and even if she did, why should I tell you, Porky? We had dinner and a few drinks, that's all. Is that okay with you dad?"

"Fine with me. Didn't you think it was strange, her being there? Didn't you stop to think about the how and the why, even for a minute?"

Now that he'd mentioned it, it was kind of unusual. How she'd found out that I'd be there, how she'd discovered where I was staying and when I was going to arrive. At the time I'd been too tired to think about it; it was nice to see a familiar face and to have someone other than Elliot to talk to. Even if she'd managed to get through to my publicists, there was no way that she would have been given that kind of information. After Lennon's assassination, the record companies became paranoid about any requests that concerned their artists. We're their property and they don't share their carrion with the other vultures. They're really anal about it, anything happens to us and they lose revenue. Sure, it's great at first, the death of a musician shifts unit sales into overdrive. Breakdowns, ODs, they're fine, but death makes the cash registers ring and fills the memorabilia stalls. Unfortunately, it's a passing fad and unless you're Elvis or Kurt Cobain, there aren't going to be any long term financial returns. Better to keep the money trickling in than blowing it in a single tax year. So, they tend to keep your movements walled up with 'eyes only' access. I've sat in meetings with the big brass and fresh faced college graduates who know as much about music as Stalin knew about the milk of human kindness, where they've asked me if I needed a bodyguard or any personal security. Seeing as how I've never had to beat the crowds off with a shitty stick, it always made me laugh and I turned their offers down. I didn't want to throw my royalties away on a steroid amped mercenary who drifted from one battle to another. So, how the fuck had Becky been able to find me?

"I didn't think. I was too tired, hungry and pissed off to go over the details."

"How about now? Now that you've had a chance to think about it Michael, doesn't it seem a little weird?"

"A little, yeah. I mean the record company wouldn't have told her, they don't know her from Adam. She could have been anyone, a freaked out stalker, a whacko, anyone. And if any of the hotel staff had blabbed, they'd have found themselves looking through the situations vacant column the next day."

"What if I told you that I knew how and why she found you?"

"Okay Sherlock, I'm all ears. Tell me how, but first tell me why. Don't elaborate or go making shit up because I can sniff a liar out faster than a frigid nun spits."

"Why, that's the easy part. Love, Michael. She loves you. Always has, always will."

"She loves me?"

"Duh! Gee Michael, you always been this naive? I thought your kind was able to latch on to women and read them like a book. Know what they want without asking."

"She loves me?"

"Yeah. What, do you need cue cards? It's a four letter word, not that hard to understand. You really had no idea?"

"No. I mean, when we were talking last night, she told me that she'd been in love with someone, said she still was. I just didn't make the connection. I thought she was talking about Elliot or maybe you or Blake. Not me, I never thought...she never said anything, didn't mention it...if I'd known..."

"You wouldn't have done anything Michael. You were too wrapped up in Alison to notice her. What was she supposed to do? Tell you and have you rip her heart out when Alison broke a nail? Some people have got more pride than that. She kept her mouth shut."

"She knew about Alison? You all knew about her?"

"Please Michael; you didn't exactly make it hard. You don't cover your tracks very well and that hangdog expression you always wore when she was around was a dead giveaway. Even Alison knew. I think she liked the way you ran after her, agreeing with anything she said."

"You got a gun Carl?"

"No Michael, this is England, we're not allowed to have them here. Why?"

"I want to blow my stupid fucking head off. No wonder she agreed to go to the reunion with me."

"Thank fuck she did. Maybe she'll shut up about you when she finds out what a wanker you really are. Maybe she'll forget about you and want to get herself a real man."

"Thanks for the encouragement Carl. It means a lot to me, knowing that you're in my corner, waving the flag and stamping on my head."

"My pleasure Michael. You haven't had to listen to her constant fucking whining. Michael did this, Michael did that, Michael was on the cover of this magazine so I bought you a copy. Michael, Michael, Michael, blah fucking blah. I won't go near her parent's house, no fucking way. It's a shrine to the life and works of one Mr. Michael Flanagan. That's some creepy shit."

I shook my head, amazed, and tried to take it all in. You do get crazy fans, now and then, sending you poetry, underwear, scabs and photographs of parts of their anatomy that you really don't want to see; the parts that should always stay private. But this wasn't some kid whose battery wasn't fully charged, it was Becky. My friend, someone I'd shared intimate, personal shit with. Not one of the psycho self-mutilation lunatics who told me that they identified with my lyrics because "Like the words, they're me man, that's my life, it's like you've always known me". Yeah, right.

"So what do you think I should do Carl?"

"Oh come on Michael, you've seen her and you're asking me what I think you should do?"

"But you said she was all spooky and shit. Obsessed and freaked out."

"I was fucking with you Michael. She's just interested in what you've been doing. I blew it up because I'm sick and tired of hearing about you and all the marvellous things you've done, the places you've seen and what not. It makes me feel like a loser, knowing that you're doing so well. It makes me feel like I've wasted my life doing something safe."

"Safe be fucked. You took the hard option, responsibility and all the scary shit that goes with it. I just got lucky."

"Whatever you want to call it, if you don't take Becky tonight Michael, I'll kick your arse. I can't take another ten years of her shit."

"Thanks Carl. How did she find me?"

"I told her Michael."

"What?"

"I told her. Soon as I found out, I went to see her and told her where you were staying and when you were arriving."

"Really? And how the fuck did you find out about it?"

"Your record label phoned and told us that you'd be in town. Thought we might be interested in making sure you were alright. Like we've got nothing better to do or we give a fuck."

Fucking humiliated. Police protection. Whoever made that call was going to get a present that they'd remember.

"How about you Carl? How's your love life?"

"I'm divorced Michael. I can't afford sex."

"Alright then. So who did you end up marrying? Do I know her?"

"Yeah, I think you might remember her. Amanda Thomas, blonde, year below us in school. Had the biggest tits you've ever seen?"

"You mean Flaps Amanda?"

"So, you do remember her then Michael?"

"Oh yeah, I remember her. Is it true?"

"Is what true Michael?"

"The reason she got her nickname. Do they dangle down to her knees?"

"Not quite down to her knees, but they're hanging there."

"That must be some sight. I wouldn't know where to begin."

"You get used to it, tweaking and tying them. There are all kinds of games you can play when your wife is blessed like she is."

"Or cursed."

"Uh huh, I guess it all depends on how you look at it. Me, I've always thought that the glass is half full and you should make the most of any situation. I did and it was a lot of fun while it lasted. When it was good, it was really good, but when it started going downhill..."

"I wouldn't know Carl. None of my relationships have lasted long enough to fall apart."

"Love them and leave them huh? Get out while there's still some light left at the end of the tunnel?"

"No, that's not it. I've never been able to give any of the women I've been with whatever it was they wanted or needed. Never been able to open up and let anyone in. After a while it became easier not dealing with it and I gave up on the relationship thing. If I've only got to worry about myself, no one can hurt me and I won't hurt anyone else. Simple mathematics. If I don't add, I can't subtract."

Carl stood, walked to the entrance of the cave and beckoned me to join him. I sighed, climbed to my feet and gave in to the smooth and sociable mature of the shingle that helped me to find my balance. He placed a hand on my shoulder and pointed out across the beach with the other.

"Look out there Michael. You see them? You see all those families? What if everyone thought the same way as you? If they did, this beach would be empty and the town would have died a long time ago. You know why they don't? Because they're not scared. They haven't backed down and given up.

Every single one of them could tell you a story about how life has tried to wear them down – tried and failed. They stood their ground and fought back, they knew somewhere inside themselves, that strength, true strength, comes with increased numbers. It doesn't matter what they do, they could be street sweepers or accountants, each one of them reflects the best part of humanity. That urge to strive for something better and they know they can't achieve that by themselves. So, they come together to create a future they can be proud of, one that doesn't have to involve greed or hypocrisy. That future is out there building sandcastles and paddling in the rock pools. Maybe they got it right and maybe they didn't, but at least they weren't scared of trying. They weren't afraid of life and when the end does come, they'll be able to hold their heads high and say that they gave it their best shot. Nobody should have to be alone Michael."

I stared out, following his finger. They were clustered together in small groups, separated by invisible lines drawn in the sand. Laughing, joking and interacting, their independence forgotten as they made the most of each passing moment. Strangers who'd gathered to collectively raise their middle digit to life and everything that it tried to throw at them. I couldn't remember seeing anything that rivalled the photogenic simplicity of the canvas Carl had laid in front of me. I gently removed his hand from my shoulder, gazed at his world one last time and turned away.

"You tried Carl and you failed. You watched your life turn to shit and walked out on your marriage. Did you fight for it?"

"Yeah Michael, I fought. But there are some battles you just can't win, regardless of how hard you fight. I didn't fail. I've got a daughter I love and who loves me without question. I may have lost the battle Michael but I won the war and that's all anyone is going to remember."

"Maybe, but I hate losing Carl and the only way you can make sure that you're not going to lose is by not fighting at all."

"I think you're making excuses. Trying to find a way to hold on to your fear and give in to it. It's time to stop being frightened and live Michael. Stop being a coward and get in the game. You owe it to yourself."

"You're right, I'm frightened. Scared of what might happen, scared that I can't predict the outcome. It terrifies me, the uncertainty, the not knowing..."

"But that's the beauty of it Michael. The uncertainty, the not knowing, that's what makes it such a challenge. Life isn't about numbers on a flow chart it's a gamble. It's about taking a risk now and then, constantly being kept on your toes, staring into the face of danger and saying fuck you. If it was pre-packaged and you knew the outcome it wouldn't be worth living. No matter what you did it wouldn't change anything. There'd be no dreams left to aspire to, no mountains left to climb, nothing would matter. For most of us, that's all they are dreams, but you...you chased yours and when you got what you wanted you stopped running. You stopped dreaming and started getting old. You've got to shake it off, start dreaming and taking risks again. Start living again."

"How?"

Taylor was laughing, wildly waving his arms around.

"I don't know Michael, it's different for everyone. I haven't got any answers, only advice. Figure out what it is you want and go for it. Seems to me that you've been handed a second chance with Becky and that's a start. Where you go from there, that's up to you."

I watched Taylor dancing, rallying against the world and was reminded of the passion the storyteller used to have. The way he drew me in, involved me in his tales, the way each of them transformed and became about me. Became personal as the third person was replaced by the first and I rode the clouds with abandon, going wherever the wind and my imagination took me. I smiled as I remembered the way my friend used to live, trawling the sea for the things he needed to sustain him, asking for nothing and expecting nothing in return; uncomplicated, unreserved and free. Freedom without a price and beyond measure. I watched as Taylor traced the shadows that lived in the cave, moving with them, their outlines blurring as they merged, then parted, the tips of their fingers lightly brushing as they courted each other in the quiet, lonely spectrum of an abandoned cave in an inconsequential hamlet. I laughed as my tears flowed and the stories flooded through me, I cried for the freedom I'd taken away and rejoiced in knowing that his spirit lived on in Taylor, Becky, Blake, Elliot, Alison and myself, lost fragments that would finally come together to make him whole; to redeem us and let us live again.

"Carl?"

His madness continued and my voice echoed unchecked through the cave. He blinked, frozen in movement, looked at me and smiled. The wide eyed smile of a child who had completely submerged himself in the game he was playing and forgotten the rude awakenings of reality.

"I'm sorry Michael, I got carried away. Sometimes I like to come here and remember the way I used to be before any of this started. To think about what it must have been like for him, living here. Forget about my life and try to live his. Man, what I wouldn't give to bring him back."

"It's okay Carl, it's okay to remember and think about him and even try to be like him. I think he would have liked that, would have liked that someone, anyone, still cared about him. That someone still cared enough about life to think of it as precious and unspoilt."

"I miss being young Michael. There isn't any mystery left in the world, everything can be explained and accounted for. All I've got is a stack of unpaid bills, a career that's going nowhere fast, an ex-wife who bleeds me dry on pay day and an overwhelming sense of paranoia that tells me I've had my time and I'm never going to get a second chance. There was so much I wanted to do, I thought I had all the time in the world and kept putting it all off until tomorrow. You know something Michael? Tomorrow never comes. It's an illusion. There's always something else to do, somewhere you have to be. Tomorrow always stops you making good on those broken promises."

He sat in the mouth of the cave and shielded his eyes from the sunlight. I crouched beside him, picked up a handful of loose pebbles and began throwing them at the rocks that were spread around us. One by one they impacted, bounced off and spun away.

"Maybe that's the way it's meant to be Carl. Maybe part of growing up is missing your youth and being able to recognise that you pissed it away. There are a million things I'd rather be doing, but it's like you said life is all about taking risks, and maybe that doesn't just apply to sex. Maybe it's a general rule that you don't learn until it's too late. I don't know I gave up trying to understand it a long time ago. The more you think about it, the more you worry about death creeping up on you and how if you don't move fast, you might as well forget it. Game over, with no extra credit. Maybe it's time to do those things you promised you would. I don't know."

"Time's catching up with us buddy and what have we got to show for it? You've got wealth and fame and I'm still here, slaving away, waiting for a break. Guess I should listen to my own advice. Stop talking, start doing and enjoy it while I still can."

"That's my boy. Get out there and give the fuckers hell."

"Seriously though Michael, did you ever think you'd make it this far?"

"Carl, after what we did that night, I didn't think I'd even last ten minutes."

"I'm not talking about that night Michael. I mean in general, did you ever think you'd make it to twenty-eight? Did you ever think about getting old?"

"I probably didn't even think about reaching twenty. They were all just numbers to me back then. Twenty five, thirty, forty, there didn't seem to be all that much difference between any of them. I guess I saw it the same way as anybody else; I'd deal with it when I got there, cross that bridge when I came to it. Did I think I'd make it? I didn't care as long as I was having a good time."

"I did. I thought I'd have made a couple of million, have a mansion, some fast cars and a beautiful wife who I'd fuck every night, rain or shine. It certainly didn't turn out like I hoped it would."

The conversation had become too morbid for my taste. I had to lighten the mood and stop dwelling on the fact that life was shit before the inevitable subject of suicide came up.

"So, who are you going to take to the reunion Carl? Who's your chosen amputee?"

"Your mother. And I'm going to bend her over, fuck her in the arse in front of everyone and whoop like a cowboy in the rodeo while doing it."

"Hmmm, given what I've heard, I think she'd like that."

We both fell into a giggling fit and sat there laughing, watching the beach.

"I don't think I'll bother going Michael. It's not the kind of thing I enjoy. Watching all those dicks I used to hate congratulating themselves on how well they've done. Besides the music is going to be fucking terrible. Can you name one decent song from back then?"

"Shake Your Foundations, AC/DC, 1985."

"Oh yeah, I can just see them cranking rock 'n' roll and dancing the night away. Do me a favour, don't be a smart arse."

"Come on Carl, you've got to go. Shit, if they ask you what you do, lie. Tell them you're a brain surgeon or some important shit like that. Women love hanging around those kind of guys, you may even get your dick sucked if you're convincing. If you get called on it, punch their lights out and move on. What are they going to do? Have you arrested?"

"It's alright for you Michael, they're all going to know who you are. Gather round you like flies to shit, wanting to crawl to the rock star. Most of them probably won't even remember my name. Or care."

"You're joking right? You think any of them give a fuck about me? They wouldn't give me the satisfaction of thinking that they care. Those tight sphincter bitches and would-be Yuppie fucks are lucky if they can make it through the day remembering their own names. Even if they don't know who you are, fuck them! School's out and they can't fuck with you anymore. The rules have changed and you're in charge now. Take your night stick and warrant card along and bust some fucking heads."

"Taking names and breaking balls, eh Michael?"

"Let my name be law and all who hear it smell fear, for they know vengeance will be mine. Alone we're nothing but together we'll crack the fucking world."

"Amen brother Flanagan."

I put my hand on his shoulder and squeezed it softly, a meaningless gesture of solidarity. The unity, and connection that I'd once felt to, and with, him was slowly returning. A fresh new breeze was sweeping through the town, its draught made my skin tingle and feel invigorated and like I was ready to remove the nails from my palms and my feet. Ready to face the constriction that had dominated and controlled my actions, ready to take my life back.

"Just what is it that you're planning to do Michael?"

"It's time to clean house Carl, get rid of the dead weight and start from scratch."

He looked at me and shrugged. Whatever he was thinking could wait. After all, time was something we had plenty of. There was enough to go around and then some.

"You know Alison is going to be there tonight don't you?"

It was a statement not a question, designed to gauge my reaction.

"I know."

"Michael if I'm stepping out of line tell me, but I've got to ask. You're not going to let her get her claws into you are you? If you are let me know because you can't string Becky along just to try to get to Alison."

"Carl, I'm seeing things more clearly than I have in a long time. Probably more clearly than I ever have. I feel like I'm finally in control and I've finally got a purpose. Flanagan's day has rolled around and nothing is going to fuck with it."

"You know that I'll run interference for you and do what I can. I want to see you happy. And I want Becky off my back."

"I appreciate that Carl. I appreciate the offer, but I've got to do my own dirty work, if I let other people do it, I'd be no better than Elliot and I'd always be relying on someone to wipe my shit away and dig me out of a ditch. If I'm going to do this, I've got to stand on my own two feet. I hope I'm strong enough to see it through, and the only way to find that out is by shutting the fuck up and doing it. Right?"

"Right. I just hope you know what you're doing."

"Carl, I haven't got a fucking clue what I'm doing. All I know is that I'm excited and a little frightened but right now, that's good enough."

"Michael you're a fucking lunatic, but if it's what you want, who am I to stand in your way? If you need me, you know where to find me."

"Yeah, propping up a bar swapping war stories with the other embittered old lushes."

"Have you been following me Flanagan? There are laws against that kind of thing. If you don't behave yourself I'm going to have to call a policeman."

I laughed, lit another cigarette and smoked, comfortable in my friend's presence. It tasted like shit. I ground it out and thought about how much I'd miss the pungent stench of tobacco and nicotine stains on my fingers. But I had to do a thorough cleaning job if I was going to pass the Flanagan inspection.

"What's the time Carl?"

He pulled a grubby sleeve back and squinted at a Casio digital watch, the kind garages give away in petrol promotions. For twenty thousand vouchers, you sir or madam can choose between an inflatable bath pillow, a superb quartz timepiece or a life size cuddly teddy bear. Thank you for your patronage, and we'll reward you with more useless tat in another sixty years. He tapped it, tilted it towards himself and cursed.

"Fucking thing, never works when you need it to. It's, uh, two twenty-seven."

Two twenty-seven. I had lots to do and the clock was ticking, counting down to the appointed hour. Time flies when you're having fun and as much fun as this was, I had to get going if I wanted to stay on schedule.

"Carl, it's been great but I've got to go. Things to do, you know how it is, life in the fast lane and all that shit. If you want to stay ahead you can't waste the day with a drunken pig in the middle of nowhere."

"If that's the way you feel Michael, fuck off, see if I care. Where are you parked? That is assuming a reprobate like you has a car."

"Oh yes, I've got a car. It's got four wheels, windows and everything. It's up on the common with the other horseless conveyances."

"Mind if I walk back with you?"

"Only if you're sure you can handle being seen with me and it won't damage your reputation too much. People will talk you know."

"Let them talk, I'm not ashamed of the way I feel. Are you, lover boy?"

"Ugh, fuck no! I'd like to think I could do better than you if I wanted to."

"What you'd like to think you can get and what you actually can get are worlds apart. Why won't you give us a chance Michael? We could be so good together, we could be featured in the celebrity centre spread of 'Hello' showing our cosy love nest off to the witless and bewildered."

"Fuck you Carl. And you say I'm the crazy one. Jesus."

"You can't blame me for trying. If you change your mind, I'll be waiting for you, lounging on a feather boa."

"Quit it will you? It's embarrassing enough as it is. If anyone ever finds out I've been hanging with the enemy, my career is fucked."

"The best way to defeat your foe is to know your enemy. They taught me that when I joined. But if you're that bothered by it maybe I should quit, open a chain of wine bars for the discerning connoisseur."

"You just don't fucking stop, do you? You've got to have the last word."

"Stay still for too long Michael and you'll get buried. Keep on moving and they'll never catch you."

As we walked toward the common, our pace slow and deliberate, we talked about the times we'd spent on the beach. The girls Carl had taken there, the beer we'd drunk and the lies we'd told in a futile attempt to impress each other. We talked about how our families used to take us down there to get some peace and a taste of freedom for just a few hours. Picnics, barbecues, any excuse to occupy the offspring with something other than television and its endless parade of puppets and talentless presenters. How our parents had, just like their children, drifted apart and barely spoke anymore, communicating through Christmas cards and chance encounters. He told me how sorry he was about my father and I accepted his commiseration, marvelling at how everyone apart from me felt genuine sorrow at his passing. How they'd cared enough to attend his send off and say goodbye. What they'd seen in the man that I hadn't, amazed me. Carl spoke of his kindness and selfless devotion to his friends and family and I listened, unwilling to shatter his illusion of the figure that he had come to see as a second father. Had I been too close to see the truth? Preferring to dwell on a teenage image of an oppressive tyrant who'd prevented my participation in the ridiculous schemes that I'd dreamt up and tried to implement on an hourly basis. Our journey ended too soon, we paused as we drew level with the hire car.

"This is me."

Carl whistled softly as he surveyed the car.

"BMW huh? I knew you were doing well Michael, but I'd no idea you were doing this well."

"It's just a rental Carl, it doesn't mean anything."

I blushed, suddenly aware of what the car represented. My ears burned as my punk sensibilities were dealt another knockout blow.

"Even so Michael, you've got to be making some money to have one of these babies waiting for you when you step off a plane."

"Put it this way, I'm not going to starve. So I'll see you tonight?"

"I guess it would be stupid to miss out and not see you for another ten years."

Jabbing the key in the lock, I turned it and heard the reassuring pop of the central locking releasing its grip.

"Somehow, I can't see that happening again. Not now anyway."

"Alright Michael, I'll catch you later. You take it easy okay?"

He hugged me with his tree trunk arms and for a brief second, I thought about asking him if he had an anchor tattoo and a cupboard full of spinach.

"Yeah, later Carl."

He let me go and started out across the common, striding purposefully away. I called after him.

"Hey Carl, is that 24 hour laundrette in town still open?"

"Yeah it's still open. I thought the hotel had a laundry, why not use that one?"

"Call it paranoia but I've had more than a few experiences with light fingered hotel staff to trust any of them as far as I could throw them."

I jumped in the car, started the engine and pulled the door shut. It roared into life straight away. Good old German engineering, built to last. Their ingenuity was going to end up shooting them in the foot, cutting the market in the quest for perfection, reducing the need to invest in a new car every few years. Buy one of their models and it will become a family heirloom, passed down from father to son as reliable as the day it rolled out of the showroom. I opened the glove compartment and took out the mobile phone our manager had insisted we bring along in case we found ourselves in the middle of some life or profit threatening emergency. They hadn't mentioned profit, but with the music business being what it was the subtext was clear and they probably had an army of trained litigators on standby ready to hush things up and make them go away. I jammed the car into reverse, spun around, slid into first and headed back into town. If they wanted an emergency I would give them one that would send their minds into overdrive and make their hair stand on end. I'd give them a crisis that would keep them in dinner invitations well into the millennium, one that would be the most popular story on the party circuit. I followed the signs for parking in the town centre and found myself turning into a multi-storey that spat its tickets out at you as you drove past and insisted that you pay on departure. And if you didn't hold on to your golden ticket, they'd cripple you with a hefty twenty-four hour charge that would break the bank of Monte Carlo.

I drove to the top level, knowing that it would be deserted, as most people are too lazy to bother with the stairs and too impatient to wait for the elevator. I picked the ticket and the mobile phone up, pulled the boot release, got out and walked round the car to gather the blanket. It felt alien as I carefully lifted it out, closed the hatch and strolled over to the chest high barrier that was supposed to stop you speeding over the edge and discourage would be jumpers and took a bird's eye view of the town to try and get my bearings. Realising where I was stunned me. The slab of concrete ugliness that I stood on had replaced the cinema in which I'd whiled away my Saturday afternoons. The place in which I'd watched effects laden blockbusters was gone, killed so that another few hundred tourists could be forced to part with their savings. I remembered the usher, the old man who had hobbled up and down the aisles trying to control the teenagers who had made the place their own and remembered the moth eaten seats, their springs bent and unravelled and the films that I used to escape into for less than the price of a packet of cigarettes. I remembered the candyfloss and popcorn that always tasted as though it had been scooped off the floor and resold. Someone had jumped the gun, torn the place down when the alarm bells about video eliminating the big screen had been rung. It was all over they'd said, why travel when you can see it in the comfort of your own home. Why bother? Missing the point had become a habit with the doomsayers. Cinema wasn't just about film. It was a universe in itself, an experience every child cherished. I wiped a solitary tear from my eye, kissed another part of my youth goodbye and took the stairs to the ground level.

The streets were bursting with locals and visitors who mixed freely as they pushed and pulled one another on their travels. With the population doubled, it was easy to blend in without attracting undue attention. I cut through an alleyway and made my way to the launderette that was hidden from all but the most inquisitive holidaymaker. Sulking in a back street, it had become a refuge for the most vocal of the locals only crew, whose membership comprised juvenile skaters and surfers. Territorial packs who guarded their hunting grounds with blood – or so they claimed. As far as I could tell, their fierce local pride amounted to nothing more than moaning and drinking. Their draught papers were available to anyone who could purchase beer without being hassled for ID.

Covered in such imaginative graffiti as 'Locals Only', the launderette hadn't changed. The crew had moved on to tagging, their bravery had increased but their spelling ability hadn't. I entered the building, a bell rang quietly and a few of the customers looked up at me and grunted in greeting, before going back to the activities that had consumed them before the warning had sounded. Top shelf pornography and right wing militaristic fiction seemed to be the latest trend to which they'd fallen victim and I returned their welcome with a curt nod.

Choosing a powder wasn't a problem. I selected one of those interchangeable brands the manufacturers claimed brought out the whitest of whites in a single wash. If you're not happy with the product they'll refund your money. Yeah and if babies grew wings they'd say they were angels. I took my powder over to an empty machine, opened it, threw the blanket in, added the powder to the waiting drawer, closed it and pressed the button that would wash my sins away, remove the stains and clean my conscience. I glanced at the clock on the wall, three-fifteen, and sat down, waiting to see if the claims were justified. I turned my attention to my cell phone; switched it on, pressed memory, saw the number flash across the screen and pressed send. I held the phone up to my ear and listened to the clicks that told me my call was being connected. Connection completed, a telephone halfway around the world began to ring. Three-fifteen here, meant it was somewhere around eight in the morning Boston time. I let it ring, not sure anyone would answer and not even sure anyone would be there. The ringing stopped abruptly and became a bright pleasant voice.

"Hello, Suffocation Management. How can I help you?"

I wondered how long it had taken her to master the phrase and make it sound as warm and appealing as it did. How long had it taken to turn the cold dread of implication into the reassuring mild greeting I had just heard?

"Is Bill Travis in yet?"

"Yes, can I tell him who it is calling and what it concerns?"

"Just tell him it's Michael Flanagan."

"I'll put you through to him now Mr Flanagan."

The line clicked again and switched to the hold muzak. I've always despised muzak, the devious insipid repetition that drains your energy and saps your will to live. When the company was up for sale, I think it was the early 90s, I'd wanted Ted Nugent's bid to succeed. Not because I like the man or agree with anything he says, I'd wanted Ted to get it purely because he said he was going to blow the motherfucking factory sky high. I prayed that they'd televise old Ted detonating the complex. When the dust eventually settled, it would have rained micro-cassettes for a month and I'd have sat there in my sunglasses, sipping a beer, giving old gun crazy Ted the thumbs up. Muzak destroys free will. That's why supermarkets are always playing it; if you can't resist, you'll buy, buy, buy. My temper started to fray as the bings and bongs tried to form some classical piece that had made the descendants of a celebrated composer beneficiaries to a fortune in back dated royalty payments. There was another click that became a booming voice.

"Hey Flanagan, how are you? Getting fat on home cooked meals?"

He sounded happy enough but there was something else there, underneath his immediate response. Panic? Worry maybe? It didn't matter. I smiled and flicked through the magazines.

"The trip was fine Bill. Listen, I've got a real problem here and need your help."

There was a drawn out pause and then he answered.

"Go on."

"This is kind of difficult so you'll have to bear with me okay? It isn't some rushed decision, I thought about it carefully before I called you, but I can't see any way out of it. It's Elliot."

"What about him Flanagan?"

"I can't work with him anymore. I can't even handle being in the same room with him anymore. One of us has got to go."

"Don't do this to me Flanagan. The album's nearly finished, the artwork is ready to go and we're already booking the tour. Please don't do this!"

"It's too late; it's out of my hands Bill. It's gone too far."

I jumped to my feet and started doing the twist to the bemusement of the other patrons.

"How can it have gone too far? I saw you guys a couple of days ago and you seemed fine..."

"Things change Bill. That's just the way it is I'm afraid. So which of us is it going to be? Who's going to get the old heave ho?"

He exploded and I had to take the phone away from my ear or be deafened. "You want me to tell you who's gonna go? Just like that with no warning?"

I imagined him sitting behind his desk, the artery in his head bubbling out of control. Any faster and it would blow out and finish him off for good.

"Yeah, that's about the strength of it. Who's it going to be? Me or him?"

"In that case Flanagan, I've got no choice, it's you. Elliot's the guy that everyone identifies with. He fronts the whole thing and gives it a human touch."

"And that's the answer you're going to go with is it Bill? That's your final word?"

"I'm sorry if it isn't what you wanted to hear Flanagan, but unless you can patch up whatever's been fucked, you've got to go."

I put the phone down on one of the chairs, gave it the bird and sniggered. I was enjoying this a little too much to hit him where it hurt. But I was going to do it anyway. I was going to punch him in his wallet and choke the cashflow.

"Flanagan are you still there? Flanagan? Are you there Flanagan?"

"Yeah I'm still here Bill. I'm sorry if that's the way you see the situation, but think about this before I hang up. Who owns all the copyright to the songs and the name of the band?"

His silence told me that I had him. It was feeding time at the zoo and boy, oh boy, were the sharks hungry. So I answered my own question.

"Bill, hey Billy boy. That's right I own them and if I go you can call it quits because I'll lawyer up so fast you won't even have time to stick that little cock of yours through the shredder. That new album you're so happy about? Forget it. That's going to be scrapped. Think about all that lovely money spent with nothing to show for it. So I'll ask you again Bill, who's it going to be, me or him?"

"We've got lawyers of our own Flanagan. We'll fight you every inch of the way."

"You're certainly welcome to try Bill, but think of the headlines. The music press will eat it up. Punk band squabbles over pennies. Imagine how disillusioned your precious kids are going to be when they read that. It doesn't fill me with confidence, what does it do for you?"

"It scares the shit out of me Flanagan. So what do you want me to do?"

"I'll tell you what you're going to do. As soon as I hang up, you're going to call the label and tell them that we had no choice but to fire Elliot and we're going to need a little more time to finish the record. Then you're going to call the publicist and have her prepare a statement, which she'll release tomorrow. Then you're going to call me back and let me know that you've done all of that, okay?"

More silence. Did he need me to spell it out for him? Send him a fax? "Then you're going to call me back aren't you Bill?"

"Yeah I can do that Flanagan. Do you want me to tell Elliot?"

"No. That pleasure is going to be mine. All mine. No more sharing."

"Okay Flanagan, I guess I'd better get on with it."

"Good boy. I won't keep you; you've got a busy day ahead."

"One last thing Flanagan. We're okay aren't we? You want to stay with us don't you?"

He was pleading. It felt good to be in charge for a change. In fact, it felt fucking perfect. I clicked my fingers and watched him jump.

"Yeah, sure, no problem. Bye Bill."

If I kept them dangling, they'd kill themselves trying to keep me happy. Let them earn their fucking money for a change. All of the magazines in the laundrette were out of date. Way, way past their interest threshold. There were a couple of articles about how the countries of the world had come to a grinding halt when Diana had died and how sad it was now that she was gone. Boo hoo, one less fucking parasite to feed. Tucked between a copy of 'Q' and a soft porn rag was a yellowing 'National Enquirer'. As I'd read more than my fair share of conspiracy theories about Elvis being held in suspended animation below the White House and how he was going to be thawed out to help Earth defeat the Martians, I tossed he Enquirer to one side and turned to watch the blanket in the machine.

I watched it tumbling around, the bloodstains leaving a rust coloured liquid as they were purified. Its colours shining as it was cleansed of the grime, the years sliding away from it. Transfixed, I watched as time flowed backwards, removing the blight that had been my conscience, my companion and my lover, the water entered each stitch and chipped away at the relationship I had refused to accept was over. As the layers were washed away, the last ten years of my life were swept before me and I wept. I wept for Flanagan who woke each morning to spend the day doing nothing more or anything less than he had the previous day. His pattern established he lived with himself, haunted by the man he should have been and knew he could be. I watched him work; crafting and writing the music that brought the dead to life and let them live vicariously, tugging at his strings, as he died each night with a smile on his face, only to have the cursed breath forced back into him each and every morning. I watched him crawl ever closer to the surface, as the layers were washed away, further and further from the fire that consumed the pit he had leapt into so many years ago.

And I wept for the youth that had been denied him, snatched away to paint a portrait of suffering for an uncaring, cruel audience; their cries of derision battering his mind as he fell further from paradise. The water was life, a new beginning, the rebirth he sought, the sorrow he carried around his neck, the brand burnt into his flesh by his own hand. As the water passed over him, he felt it enter his mouth, tasted its salvation, its opportunity. Felt the water as his scars drew in on themselves and the new flesh that lay beneath them, pink and raw, felt the air, felt the pollution and became firm. His fingers broke the surface and he felt the droplets roll from his face, felt the water breathe new life into the diseased sacks that kept him alive. I watched as the water drained away and left a blanket, a blanket that had once been used by an old man to ward off the long winter nights. A blanket that had been a shroud, a shooting gallery and a friend in the hours of darkness. Its cycle finished, the machine shuddered to a halt, I opened the door and allowed my hands to venture in. I stroked its soft alien hide and lifted it from its chamber and placed it in the dryer. Feeding the coins into the slot, I made sure that the machine's belly was full before starting it up and as the blanket rolled from side to side in the barrel, I picked up the 'National Enquirer' and lost myself in its lurid stories about an American tourist discovering Noah's Ark in the Rocky Mountains, Jesus being reborn to lead the African nations and how the missing link had set up home in the Himalayas. And as I read, I waited for the phone to ring.

5:17 P.M. August 29th, 1998

By the time I left the launderette, the National Enquirer had convinced me that Jimmy Hoffa was still alive and was now the head of covert operations for the militia groups that were spreading across America. The phone hadn't rung, but that was okay, Bill was dealing with it, which was, after all, what I was paying him for.

The temperature dropped, falling to the point where it was comfortable to stroll through the streets in a t-shirt, without sweating and the crowds had thinned out, their pace had eased and their mood changed. No longer anonymous, the pack turned their attention toward me, focusing on the carnival attraction that carried a blanket in his tattooed arms. Leering, whispering and shaking their heads, I let them stare; let them find some amusement and small pleasure in my appearance. If I was abhorrent to them, I was noticed and not hidden away like the dirty secret my life had become. As I walked among them, they stepped away from me, giving me the space I needed to continue, the room I needed to be to live and to be. They pulled their children to one side as I passed them, warning them that if they didn't behave they'd end up like me, singled out and despised. Their jeers heightened my resolve, added to my strength and I hurried back to the car, a manic grin fixed in place. The phone rang as I was unlocking the door, and casually flipping the blanket onto the back seat, I answered it.

"Yeah, Bill it's me."

"Okay Flanagan they all went for it. I wouldn't say they were ecstatic about the situation, but they seemed to handle it pretty well. One condition though. They want you back in the studio next week to re-track the vocals, and it's got to be you or the whole deal is off."

"That's fine Bill, I'll be there on Monday. We're going to need another guitarist."

"You got anyone in mind Flanagan?"

"Uh huh, give Charlie from Monster Box a call. He's a good guy and he's been having a rough ride with the rest of the band. I reckon he's looking for an excuse to bail and this is a perfect opportunity for him."

"Alright Flanagan, if you want him, I'll get him."

"Thanks Bill. I'll see you and Charlie next week then?"

"We'll be waiting for you. I'll keep the champagne on ice"

"Sounds like a date."

He was laughing when I clicked the phone off and threw it on top of the blanket. Not bad, in less than two hours I'd ripped my manager's world apart. Just goes to show what you can do when you put your mind to it. I'd had him running scared and too frightened to take his foot off the pedal for an instant. In a perverse kind of way, I think he enjoyed fucking Elliot over almost as much as I did. I'd let him flex his wasting muscles and join the beat-down instead of being a spectator. I drove out of the car park, left the crumbling buildings behind and joined the newly constructed by-pass that had been laid over the country lanes I'd ridden through on my bicycle as a child.

I thought about buying some more cigarettes and tried to resist the sweet cries of the nicotine that raged through my veins, tried to tell myself that I was shit out of luck and if I wanted them that badly I'd have to go back into town, a drooling fool who freely admitted to being a slave to the acceptable face of addiction. I didn't have enough time to swing around to feed my lust and battered it down with the promise that I'd lovingly tend to its call when I could. It's refusal to listen turned the car onto a garage forecourt, marched me by the scruff of the neck to the service window and instructed the clerk to hand over three packs of the nearest brand. My addiction wasn't bothered by taste or aroma and as long as the necessary chemicals were present, it didn't give a fuck about tar percentage. Gathering my change, I gazed at the sun as it dipped below the horizon, leaving a red hue in its wake as the daylight started to fade.

I got back into the car and switched the radio on, scanning through the stations, but they all sounded the same. They all pumped out the same lethargic, tired shit that had made music stale and boring and I gave up trying to find a DJ who would take a risk and play a tune that hadn't been pre-approved by is bosses and placed on heavy rotation. Lighting up, I got back on the by-pass and gunned the engine, urging the car on. The journey was longer than I remembered it being and it seemed to take an eternity to reach the cemetery gates and one of its few spaces. There was a multi-storey for the living and a tiny allocation for the dead. Almost as if they were an afterthought, which was, all things considered, strangely fitting.

Picking the blanket off the seat, I left the car and walked toward the gate, its hinges were rusted and groaned as I pushed it open. It was a simple plan, find his grave, lay the blanket on it, get back in the car and head back to the hotel. Easy. Taylor had been right; his mausoleum was impossible to miss and towered above the indistinguishable stones that marked the dates and memories of the little people who surrounded him. Sighing, I struck out alone to talk to my mentor, to tell him what he'd meant to me, return his property and ask for his forgiveness. A woman knelt in front of his marble epitaph and laid flowers at its base, one hand lightly stroking the stone marker. I shuffled forward awkwardly, as waking the dead was the last thing I wanted to do. She turned and looked up at me, her surprise giving way to disdain as she stared at my shirt and tattoos. She was younger than me, maybe twenty-four, twenty-five, but her blue eyes burned with the cold fire of authority and the black void of power.

"Who are you? What do you want?" she snapped.

What does anybody want in a graveyard? What business does any living soul have with the departed? I'd come here to gloat, to remind the residents of what they once had, remind them what it was they had lost and what had been taken from them.

"I've, uh, come to pay my respects," I replied, unable to meet her stare.

"You're a little bit late for that aren't you? Did you know my father or are you just another employee pretending to care hoping to score some points at the next board meeting?"

Her father? So this was the daughter who had opened Pandora's Box and broken the seal I'd fought so desperately to fasten. I felt the colour drain from my cheeks and my hands start to shake.

"Sort of," I said nervously when I managed to catch my breath.

"Sort of? What kind of answer is that? You either did or you didn't. Which one is it?"

Oh I knew him alright, I'm the reason he's lying under our feet. He's dead because I couldn't keep a secret. Couldn't keep my mouth shut.

"I knew your father," I sighed, pointing at his resting place. "But I didn't know that he was rich, I didn't know that side of him."

"So how did you know him then?" she demanded.

"As a lonely old man who lived in a cave on the beach."

"I'm so sick of you people, thinking you can ease your conscience by visiting his grave. Thinking you can make up for what you did to him as children. You should have thought about what you were doing then, not now."

"What?" I gulped, nearly falling against the statue.

"I've heard the stories, I know about how you all used to throw stones at him, how you used to make fun of him when he was alive. It's too late to say you're sorry. If he jumped off that cliff, it was you who drove him to it. So just leave."

I'd thought she knew, knew what I'd done to him, how I'd bundled him up and thrown him into the sea. She'd assumed I was here to ease my conscience, and she was right, but for all the wrong reasons. She was sharp, I was the right age group and didn't exactly look like I was overburdened by compassion. I could easily have been one of the thugs who had tormented him and chased him from one end of the beach to the other.

"Wait a minute. Slow down, you've got it wrong. That's not the reason I'm here at all," I said, as she turned her back on me. "I didn't do any of those things."

"You didn't?" she asked quietly, turning to face me again.

"No I didn't, but I understand how you might think I did."

"Then why are you here?"

"Because he was my friend. One of my only friends."

"He was your friend?" she asked, mystified.

"Yeah, I used to go to his cave and he'd tell me stories, and I'd just sit there and listen. They were some of the happiest times I ever had, sitting there, listening to him."

"My father told you stories? What kind of stories?"

"It's hard to put into words. They were exciting, amazing and wonderful. About the closest I can come to explaining them, is they were like fairy tales, you know? There were always good guys and bad guys, they were always fighting over something or other, I don't know, they were just...incredible."

"He talked to you? What was he like?"

"He was just a nice old man, someone who would always talk to you."

She sighed.

"All I know about his life here is what I've been told by the locals and all they remember is the old drunk who lived by the sea."

"Oh no," I smiled "He was far more than that. At least he was to me."

"I never knew him," she whispered. "He left just after I was born; all I know is that he was good at what he did and that he liked to drink. Not a lot is it? Not a lot to try to get to know someone from, is it?"

"No it isn't, but they were only a part of him and they're not the parts I remember."

When she smiled, the fire in her eyes died.

"I'm glad that you remember him fondly. It's nice that someone does."

As we stood by the grave, I remembered the blanket and handed it to her.

"I think he would have wanted you to have this."

"What is it?"

"Something he gave me a long time ago. Something he reluctantly gave to a cold frightened lonely boy."

She took it in her hands and held it up to her face, burying it in the blanket's soft surface. She held it the way I used to, finding solace in its smooth surface. The seconds dragged out and I began to think that she'd never let go, never release the only tangible memory she had of a man who was unknown to her. I wondered what she was thinking, trapped in the blanket's misery. If only she could have seen what it had seen, the life it had been a part of for so long, and the life it had been forced into. Lowering it to her chest, she studied me and tried to understand why I'd given her the only part of my friend I had left.

"He gave this to you?" she asked, her hands following the lines that had been folded into the blanket.

"Yes, he did, and now I'm giving it to you."

"Why? Why give it to me now?"

Why? Because I didn't need it any more. Because a friend made me realise that while it's okay to remember the past, if you live in it you stagnate and you'll never achieve all the magnificent things you dreamed about when you were young. Because I didn't want to live in that cold dark cave any longer, I didn't want to hate the sound of the waves and I didn't want them to haunt my dreams. I wanted to face up to my life and own it for myself. Because...

"Because we have more in common than you know."

"We have?" she retorted. I nodded.

"My father's buried here as well, somewhere out there," I finished, and pointed in the general direction of the headstones that surrounded us.

"You don't know where?" she asked incredulously.

"No, I've got no idea. This is the first time I've been back in ten years. I didn't even go to his funeral. I couldn't see any reason to."

"Then why come here now?"

"Maybe it's just the right time," I said. "Or it could be that I was wrong about him, he wasn't the monster I thought he was and it's time to make peace and let my ghosts rest."

"I wish I could let go," she sighed. "I wish I could accept the way he died, but with solicitors involved it's damn near impossible."

"What the hell have lawyers got to do with your father's death? It was more than a decade ago, he slipped on the rocks and drowned," I said, vaguely hoping she'd open up and let me know what was really going on.

Lawyers? Why the fuck would they still be sniffing around? And why had she had the case reopened?

"Slipped or pushed?" she sighed.

"Pushed? Why would anyone have wanted to do that? It doesn't make sense."

"It doesn't make any sense to me either, but while there's an element of doubt, they're going to chase after this thing."

"Take it from someone who knows. I can't think of anyone who would have done something like that. So kids throw stones at him and called him names? That doesn't mean they wanted to kill him. They were just young, foolish and scared."

That wasn't exactly true, I could think of one sorry excuse for a human being that would happily have done it. But he'd keep until later and stay on ice until I was ready to thaw him out, skewer him and slowly roast him over the fire he'd spent the last ten years stoking.

"And you don't think that fear isn't motivation enough for murder?"

"Is that what you really think? You think your father was murdered?"

Her shoulders slumped and she suddenly looked incredibly tired. She looked like she'd been carrying the weight of the world and couldn't go any further.

"No, but while the company solicitors are fighting over his insurance settlement it's never going to end, so what I think is irrelevant."

"Insurance settlement?"

I shouldn't have started digging. I didn't know how deep this hole was going to end up being.

"That's what it all comes down to, his insurance settlement. While he was still running the company, my father took out a life insurance policy that he made sure was paid up in full that included a wrongful death clause. If they can prove there's a case to answer, the pay out doubles."

Money? It was all about money? Why did everything always end up being about money?

"And the payment is worth dragging this thing on for is it? Is that what it's about for you? Money?"

"No. No amount of money could ever replace him but it's all gone too far to stop now. I've got to see this thing through to the bitter end."

I knelt down, and tugged at the grass.

"I'm no expert on these kinds of things," I began, "but it seems to me that the only people who are bothered about how he died are these lawyers of yours. They're the ones who can't accept it, and they never will. For them it's a win-win situation. You keep paying them to push for this huge settlement that they are undoubtedly going to get a percentage of. All they can see are pound signs and as long as it's going on, you're right – it's never going to end. Maybe it's time for you to let go as well. Let go and let your father rest in peace."

"What can I do though?" she wailed.

"These lawyers, they work for your company don't they?"

"That's right; they handle all the corporate litigation as well as the personal cases."

"And, correct me if I'm mistaken, you're the head of the company, the big cheese, the one in charge?"

She smiled.

"Yes I'm, the chief executive, or the big cheese as you put it so eloquently."

"Then why not fire them and drop the case?" I said bluntly.

She shook her head.

"If I was to fire them without a reason, I'd be the subject of one of their lawsuits. They've tasted blood and they want more."

I nodded.

"Since I've been back here, I've learned a couple of important lessons and one of them springs to mind. If there's one thing that people in power are afraid of more than anything else, it's the thought that someday they might lose that power."

I thought about Bill sitting behind his desk in Boston, swallowing one pill after another, trying to keep his blood pressure down.

"Threaten them with that loss and they become pussy cats. It knocks them for six, leaves them confused and while they're chasing their tails you pounce and pound on them until the message becomes clear. They'll soon start taking you seriously."

She thought about what I'd told her, toyed with it for a while and then asked, "What if they don't? I don't know if I can take the risk."

"Listen lady, where I live the legal system has got an answer for everything. It's the pot of gold at the end of everybody's rainbow. If they don't go for it, threaten them with a countersuit, one that will make them shit pink."

"What can I sue them for? They've got me for unfair dismissal and breach

103

of contract."

"How about mental anguish? Keeping you in suspense for ten years and not allowing you to close the book on your father. That's as good a place to start as any. Get yourself another lawyer and see what they've got to say about it. If there's one thing those guys love, it's going after their own kind. It sharpens their claws and puts them in the right mood for the kill."

"Set a thief to catch a thief?" she grinned.

"Exactly."

"Just who the hell are you?" she whispered.

Michael, my name is Michael and I'm home.

"Does it matter who I am? I'm nobody. An old friend repaying a debt."

Whether she understood or not, I'll never know. I'd like to think she did and I hope she knew that it was fate giving both of us a wake up call.

"Well whoever you are Mr Nobody, consider your account paid in full."

She reached out to shake my hand, I accepted and smiled.

"Why did you stay after I asked you to leave?"

Because life was about taking risks and if you didn't fly close to the edge now and again, you'd never know what it was you stood to lose.

"I thought you looked like you needed to talk."

"Maybe we both did. Whatever your reason, I'm glad you did. You know, I've been coming here most days for the last five years and you're the only person I've talked to who had anything pleasant to say about my father."

"He was a good man. Remember that. Hold onto that thought and everything else will take care of itself."

She nodded and glanced down at her watch.

"I'm sorry, I've got to go, being the...how did you put it? The big cheese, if I don't crack the whip they'll think I've gone soft. Can I give you a lift somewhere?"

"No, I think I'll stay a while.""Have it your way. It was nice to meet you Mr Nobody. Maybe I'll see you again?"

"I don't think so."

"Well if I don't, I hope you find whatever it is you're looking for."

"Maybe I already have."

Maybe it'd been here, right in front of me all the time and I just needed somebody to point it out to me.

Being right about a situation or a person doesn't make you feel any better about yourself. Every time you hit the nail on its head, strike it home, a piece of you dies inside. Withers away with the predictability that manages to tear its way through space, finality and matter. Our paths didn't cross again. I read about her exploits, the deals she struck, the economies she revitalised and I felt the pride that I knew should have been her father's. I wondered if she ever thought about the tattooed stranger she'd talked to in the cemetery that evening. If she did, I hope that she kept a good thought for him, because fuck knows karma is hard to come by and most of us need all the luck we can get. As she left, I read the inscription on the faceplate sealed in the statue. Robert Townsend, 1930-1988. Brief and to the point. No quotes, no biblical passages, just a name and a date. Robert, Bobby, Bob, I tried all the variations and none of them worked. Putting a name to his face took away the magic and made him human, just another lost soul wading through the shit with the rest of us, confused, frightened and alone. I leaned against the marble, felt the cold winter of the grave.

"I'm sorry Robert. I'm sorry for what happened and wherever you are, I hope you can find some measure of forgiveness for me. Goodbye old friend, I miss you."

I could have chosen to take the path back to the car, but I wanted to explore, hoped that by chance I'd fortuitously stumble across the marker I was really looking for. Somewhere in the middle of this stone forest was my pop, sleeping through his days and nights, rising out of the ground once a year, wearing a plastic cape and fake fangs, on Halloween to lecture any of the local kids who'd been brave enough to sneak in to drink their liquor on the logistics and marvels of mechanical engineering. I hoped that whoever had the plot next to him had paid their bills promptly, voted conservative and didn't like to argue. If they hadn't there would be no eternal rest for them, they'd spend infinity fending off vocal attacks from their noisy neighbour.

I searched through the names, the children and the adults who had lived, worked, played and died in the town and become part of its ambience when their usefulness had ended. Strangulation, electrocution, cancer, natural causes, there were so many ways to go and each of them had been tried and tested by the inhabitants. Seven thousand down, twenty three thousand to go. I couldn't find him, couldn't pinpoint his position. I sat down, leaning against a stone that told anyone who cared how dangerous it was to fuck around with guns. Maybe it wasn't important, finding his plot. Maybe all that was important was that I was there. If he was listening, and not too busy getting off on the sound of his own voice, he'd hear me no matter where I was. I inhaled and said what I'd come to say.

"Hey dad. I hope you can hear me, because this is the only time I'm going to say it. I'm not going to repeat myself so listen up. I was wrong and I'm sorry. That doesn't mean you were right. We both made mistakes and who was right and who was wrong doesn't matter anymore, but for whatever it's worth, I'm sorry."

I tilted my head and listened for the faint 'I told you so' that I was sure would follow. I waited for a response and when none came, shrugged, smiled and headed for the gate. The car was where I'd left it and hadn't fallen prey to the desires of a teenage delinquent who fancied the idea of a future in formula one and wanted to get in as much practise as he could before his seventeenth birthday. I climbed in, popped a tape in the stereo and listened to The Accused plough through 'Psychomania', trying to decipher whatever the heck it was that Blaine Cook was screaming about for the three hundred and seventy-seventh time. I gave up, started the car and headed back to the hotel, making up lyrics about zombies being harvested by Doctor Phibes and the Legions of Hell so that they could open a holiday camp while Blaine and his cohorts thrashed through the song.

Pulling into the car park, I grabbed the mobile and briskly made my way through the creaking revolving doors of the hotel and up to reception. It was deserted. Again. These people really knew how to keep their customers happy. Make the customer grin and bear it. Some easy listening tune had been left on a continuous loop and I considered mounting the desk and ripping the speakers out of the walls and killing that shit deader than a week old cadaver. Instead I struck the bell repeatedly, stopping when a faint aroma hit my nostrils, the sickly, almost sweet smell of home grown weed that was followed by the hushed cursing of a desk jockey who'd been disturbed by my arrival. Rushing around the partition, he lost his footing a couple of times and slid into place, grace and dignity abandoned as he resumed his duty. He was out of breath and his eyes were glazed.

"Yes sir, how can I help you?" he panted.

"Flanagan, room 35. I'd like my key."

"Yes sir."

He turned, searched through the alcoves that had been cut from the partition and numbered in sequential order. Finding the right one, he removed the key and removed the slips of paper it had been resting upon.

"You've got four messages. One from a Mr Elliot Kuntz..."

"Kurtz. It's Kurtz." I interrupted.

"Yeah, Kurtz, that's it," he said squinting at the note, and realising what he'd said started to apologise. "I'm so sorry Mr Flanagan, it's the writing. I'm really sorry," he repeated.

"That's alright, he is a kuntz, don't worry about it," I smiled.

"Who left the other three?"

"The other three? Oh right, the messages. Uh they're all from a Miss Becky Connolly."

"Thank you," I said, taking the paper from him. "Do you mind if I make a suggestion?"

"No sir," he replied. "Management always welcomes any suggestions that our guests feel would be appropriate, or would improve the service."

It was a simian response to a sapien's question. Training them up before packing them off to the war zone increases their chances of survival.

"If you're going to smoke that shit, do it away from work and you might stay lucky."

He gulped and began babbling.

"It was so quiet, I was bored...I didn't expect anyone to be back this early. I won't happen again, I promise."

"Relax, I'm not going to rat you out, if you can get paid to put your feet up, just expect the unexpected okay?"

"Yes sir, I'll keep that in mind."

'Sir', man did I eat that shit up, tell me more sunshine. I left him to contemplate the lesson of the day and wondered if he knew how close he'd come to having his nuts squeezed in a vice. Smoking grass in the workplace. The kid was a genuine subversive; either that or he really was bored out of his fucking skull. Eight hours a day of 'Where's my sea view? I paid for a view of the sea and not the main road', and 'How long does it take to make a cup of coffee?', would do that to you, would leave you with a head full of sludge, and turning the tap off wasn't an option when you were sitting behind the counter. Still, he'd been smoking some good shit, not the oregano that the Kerouac Appreciation Society had poured into the universities and technical colleges that were dotted all over the land. I despaired of the future, a place where no one could tell if they were toking on kitchen herbs or hydroponic miracle grow. Where getting high was something your parents used to do when they were young. The more I thought about it, the more the future seemed a barren place, where fun had been outlawed and productivity was the new religion. A church devoted to industry and the commandments of capitalism. Heaven meant having a seat on the board and a place at the exchange and unemployment was original sin, where no amount of Hail Mary's or rosaries could buy you out of hell. Without drugs to get through that crap, you may as well just stick your head in the oven and turn the gas on.

I scanned the messages and decided to call Becky on the mobile, rather than have the hotel charge international rates for a local call. I crumpled Elliot's message up and threw it over my shoulder, letting it bounce down the stairs. I opened the door to my room, read the number, switched the mobile on and called. She picked up after the second ring. She must have been sitting next to it chewing her nails, begging and pleading with it to ring. If the phone would just ring, she'd give to charity; devote herself to a life of chastity and good deeds. I'd done the same thing too many times to believe that that I was the only one who did it and that it was a unique, solitary neurosis.

"Hello."

"Hey Becky, it's Michael. I'm returning your call."

"Hi Michael. I just wanted to make sure you remembered you're supposed to be picking me up tonight."

"Doctor Connolly, I'm shocked. Of course I remember. What do you take me for?"

"Well you were pretty blasted last night."

"Blasted perhaps. But I'd never forget asking a beautiful woman out for an evening of wine and song. What did you say that Swedish friend of yours was called? Helga, Olga, the one you said was game for anything?"

"Very droll Michael. You sound happy, what's wrong?"

"Nothing. I've been a busy beaver, putting the world to rights."

"Want to tell me about it?"

"Not yet, you'll find out later."

"You promise?"

"Scout's honour."

"I didn't know you were in the scouts Michael. Have you still got the uniform?" "I might have."

"Hmmm, maybe you'll put it on for me sometime..."

I usually had to pay women to talk dirty to me, using those sex lines that root your call through half of the capital cities of Europe. But I'd maxed my credit cards out, pushed them to their limit trying to reach orgasm from the back of a tour bus. In all probability, while I'd been whacking off to a mental image of Jane Weidlin, I'd been talking to Mabel, a retired librarian from Bumfuck, Idaho. When you're lonely and a long way from home, with no end in sight, a friendly voice can mean the difference between sanity and the welcoming chasm of madness. At least, that was the way I'd justified the most expensive dates I'd ever had that all ended the same way – alone with my dick in one hand and a box of Kleenex in the other.

"Look Becky, I got to cut and run. Grab a shower and get into my monkey suit." "
Alright Michael, I'll see you in a couple of hours."

"You bet."

She hung up and I was left holding the phone, shaking my head in wonder. Why she would still want me after I'd skipped out and forgotten she'd even existed was beyond my comprehension. I tried to contain my excitement, told myself that Taylor had been winding me up, setting me up for a fall and that I'd finish the evening with egg on my face, jerking off in my hotel room. Still I couldn't get rid of the thought that maybe this was something even I couldn't fuck up. That Flanagan's curse had been broken and I'd end up winning one, not limping home jiggling my keys. Hope springs eternal and I was becoming a firm believer in the age-old adage that all things came to those who wait. After standing patiently in line, I could smell the future and from the tiny sample I'd had, I knew the chef was cooking up a storm.

The tuxedo that the record company had delivered and the staff had been kind enough to bring up to my room was lying on the bed. I unzipped the covering sheet and smiled. It was exactly what I'd asked for. Velvet frills and wide collars with the sleeves removed from the jacket and shirt. The label had probably popped a couple of fuses to accommodate me, but I was the 'artist' and if I wanted something, they had to deliver – period. No more convoluted stories or excuses. I figured that if I was going to cover my arms with tattoos I wasn't going to keep them to myself. They had taken years of painful surgery to complete, joining the dots and colouring the gaps. In the right kind of light they were almost tasteful. Not worthy of critical praise and definitely not as close to perfection as the field would ever come, but I'd grown used to them. I've always said that getting tattooed was a little like losing your virginity. Before you get down to it, you hear a lot of talk about what it's like, opinions that run the gamut from the factual to the absurd. The only thing that is true is that it's just as compulsive as sex. Once you've had a bite you want more and the more you get, the more adventurous you become. Instead of the self-inflicted scrawls that ex-cons wear so proudly, you'll want a full back piece that depicts the knights of Arthurian legends or the DC superheroes whose exploits filled listless, rainy Sunday afternoons of your childhood. Over time, the relationship you develop with your tattoo artist is the same as you forge with a girlfriend. You put your trust and implicit faith in them. Except most tattoo artists are fat, bald men, but if that's what set your sails at full mast, then so be it.

I took a quick shower and put the hotel's courtesy cosmetics in my bag when I dried myself off. If it's free, I'll take it. I had a drawer full of the shit at home. I didn't use it; I just liked to know it was there. I tried on the tuxedo. The trousers were a perfect fit. My waist size has stayed pretty constant, its spread kept in check by the way I fling myself around the cardboard stages we've always been booked to play. Work out with Flanagan and you'll feel the difference. Fight that flab and sing along. It's easy, jump, stretch and repeat ad infinitum. I checked the time and having an hour to spare picked up the channel guide to see what the hotel had laid on to encourage its guests to use room service. Deciding to go with the adult channel wasn't hard. It was either that or be subjected to the drivel that another action hero spouted as he offed bad guys and tried to rescue some maiden who'd found herself caught up in their evil schemes via a series of preposterous plot twists and developments. Tutting to myself I watched the actors and actresses go through the motions, simulating sex in a dentist's waiting room. Nobody seemed to enjoy their work anymore. Sure, they grunted and groaned in all the right places but something was missing. Porn hasn't been the same since the 80s, when all the real stars decided that they wanted to become legitimate thespians, respected for their minds as well as their bodies. Porn had become like music, stale, mainstream and safe; an industry where profit was found in imitation rather that innovation.

Music hadn't been a threat since Derby Crash had died and porn had never recovered from the Traci Lords' scandal. They were both content to tread water, rehashing old ideas, giving them a slightly different slant and selling them to the youth that the market was dealing with in increasing numbers. Musicians and porn stars are drawn to each other, it's the closest one comes to wonderful depravity and the other comes to crossing over to a wider audience. I'd been concentrating on one actress for too long and had missed the gradual slide, the slow decline in its standards and considered myself

110

lucky that I had. If this plastic copy of its glory days was what the directors and producers were pedalling then I could cope well enough without it. The hunger had gone and having too much respect for its pioneers, I switched the television off and left Dick and Jane to play out their fantasy for someone else.

I checked the contents of my bag. Hidden underneath the shirt where I'd stashed it, was my dope. It seemed a shame to flush it. There was close to a grand's worth of gear left, and I'd always been told that money didn't grow on trees and wasting it was an act of the foolhardy, those who didn't give a damn about the consequences of their actions. Stick it in my arm or rid myself of another crutch? It was a dilemma alright and I considered the arguments for and against it, the pros and cons. I listened diligently to both sides. In the end it came down to a new start, so I strolled to the toilet, poured the contents into the bowl and flushed the lever whilst pissing on the powder that had clung to the rim. I returned to the suite, sat on the bed and studied my invitation.

'Dear Friend'. Not the way I'd have phrased it but I hadn't sent them out. 'Do you ever think about your school days?' No. I'd made it my prerogative to do that as little as I could. 'And the times we had together? Have you ever wondered what happened to the pupils of yesterday?' No, although privately I'd wished they'd all choked on shit. 'And the people they became? Ten years is a long time...' – wasn't fucking long enough – '...and even though it only seems like yesterday since we walked those hallowed corridors together, time has passed us by. So we invite you to relive those days with a 1988 class reunion. Feel free to bring your partners and spouses and introduce them. See you there.'

Whoever had the clever idea of throwing this shindig had printed their request on cheap yellow card with a tacky purple border. It made me nauseous just looking at the fucking thing, let alone reading and complying with it. However, the life of a 'celebrity' is a hectic one, hopping with the jet set and their ilk, and so here I was, ready to dazzle my old "friends" with my gracious presence and lie about how many super models I'd slept with, three in a bed romps, twelve day amphetamine marathons and any other horseshit I could think up on the spur of the moment. As soon as the publicist had told me that I was going and didn't have a say in the matter, I'd made up my mind and decided that whatever happened, I was determined to have a thoroughly miserable time and act like the punk rock caricature that everyone expected me to be, aloof, obnoxious and a real prick to boot.

Now though, I wasn't sure that was the right thing to do. Although what the right thing was, I wasn't exactly sure of either. I looked at the bedside clock – 8:07 – I was already late. I pocketed the invitation and shrugged it off. I'd be fashionably not on time, that's what the magazines had called it in one of those articles that talked about the right and wrong ways to behave at social gatherings. You had to play it cool, and arrive somewhere in the middle of late and early, hoping to fuck that you'd timed it right. Fuck. Thanks to reading articles like that, I'd even discovered where the clitoris was and how to stimulate it; in theory anyway. Putting it into practise was a different matter. According to the plethora of gossip magazines I'd consumed while stranded in the back of a tour bus and slowly dying a little more every day, it was all about circular motion, going around it and never touching it directly. Round and round it goes, where it stops no one knows, which I thought was sort of ironic and a little too close to home, and my life story, for comfort.

Slamming my room door behind me, I ran for the stairs not wanting to be too late. I pulled up outside Becky's parents' house and realised how nervous I really was. It felt like my first date all over again and I remembered the hell that had been. All I'd wanted was a quick fumble, something that would prove I wasn't, as my dear old school chums delighted in calling me, a 'fag'. I was fourteen years old and she was one of the girls that used to hang around a small cafe in town, smoking cigarettes that she'd stolen from her mother the night before. I knew her by reputation rather than name and was desperate to find out whether her nickname had been earned through a love of chocolate or how far she'd let you go, after all Kit Kat was kind of open to any number of possibilities. I knew which one I believed and that was all I cared about. One of my brother's friends who used to let me borrow his records had told me it was because she took two fingers.

"Two fingers?"

I'd asked the question in innocence and he laughed and said that I should think about it. Which I did and when I realised what he was talking about, my grin made him laugh even harder. We ended up going to see one of Arnie's mid-eighties law enforcement flicks at the cinema that eventually became a multi-storey. I thought it was a celluloid slab of fucking righteous hard line justice, but she just sat there chewing the same piece of fucking gum, not talking, just chewing that fucking gum. After the film finished, I thought I'd blown my chances. If she'd wanted to reveal her secret to me she'd have done it inside where all the other couples did, so I walked her home and about three hundred yards away from where her parents were sleeping, she pulled me into an alleyway and pounced. My brother's friend had been well informed.

I walked down Becky's driveway and knocked on her door, whistling the theme to James Bond, a secret agent dressed to kill in his evening wear. A pimp's fedora would have been a nice finishing touch but I never did have an eye for detail. Her father answered and stared at me. Becky must have said something to him, told him to be on his best behaviour. It took him a while to smile, but he made it in the end.

"Hello Michael. Do you want to come in for a minute? Becky's still getting ready; you know what women are like?"

Uh, no, I don't as it happens. Any chance you could tell me, give me some advice.

"If you don't mind Mr. Connolly?"

"My bank manager calls me Mr. Connolly, we're both adults, call me John. Come in."

He showed me into the lounge and we sat opposite each other, smiling inanely. A clock was ticking in the background and each second was a hammer fall. We didn't speak, and sat there grinning in silence. I knew what he was thinking. The unspoken warning all fathers give to their daughter's prospective suitors.

"I've warned her about you. About your nasty little ways. As soon as you try anything she'll be ready. If you do manage to have your wicked way, I'll know. The minute she comes through the door, I'll know. I'll be able to smell it and then I'll come looking for you with a few of my friends. And we'll bring our guns, some knives and a gallon of petrol. When we find you, we'll have us a lynching party. They'll see the flames for miles around."

I heard a thumping and some muttered cursing from the hallway, and prayed it was Becky and that she was ready to leave. Ready to get out of the house and away from her father, away from the stare that was boring into my skull. She poked her head round the doorframe and smiled. She had tied her hair back into a ponytail and wore a low cut ball-gown. Her pale skin shone in the soft hue of the room's illumination.

"Hi Michael, are you ready?"

"Yeah, I'm ready any time you are."

"Great. Let's make a move then shall we?"

Her father followed me over to the door, not quite ushering me out but making sure I left nonetheless. Becky had already left the house and I joined her feeling his stare as he watched every move I made.

"You look fabulous."

I know it's what you're meant to say, even if it isn't true. I wasn't lying. She looked majestic. The most beautiful woman I'd ever seen and believe me there's a lot of good looking girls working in pornography. She looked at me and giggled.

"And you look like a clown. It isn't fancy dress you know?"

"Are you sure? I could have sworn that's what it said on my invitation."

"Let's just go shall we?"

"If madam would care to accompany me, her chariot awaits."

"Why thank you kind sir."

I walked up the drive and felt her father's eyes burrowing into my back. I turned to see him nod, a gesture that I was all too familiar with.

"You remember what I told you young fella. I'll know, just you see if I don't."

I was the perfect gentleman as we got into the car, because I knew that if he saw me make a single mistake, my arse would be history, and he was a patient man who was just waiting for me to slip up. We were half way there before I relaxed, satisfied that John was no longer watching me.

"Becky, is your dad always that intense?"

"Only when it comes to the men who take his daughter out."

"Especially if they look like they should be serving thirty years for fratricide, right?"

"That's one way of looking at it. Don't take it personally; you're a lot to take in at once. I'm surprised he invited you in, he usually leaves people on the doorstep."

"And you didn't tell him to go easy on me?"

"Was it that obvious? Subtlety never was one of his strong points."

"It could have been worse, he could have strip searched me or made me fill out a questionnaire. I guess if I'd been in his place and I turned up, I'd have locked the family silver away and pretended that I had the wrong address."

We arrived at the crossroads that separated her estate from the main road; I indicated right and pulled out almost immediately. I'd forgotten how quiet these streets became at night. How life was a nine to five occupation and after clocking out you sealed yourself up in your private hole.

"Are you going to tell me?"

"Tell you what?"

"What it is that's made you so pleased with yourself?"

"I already told you. I've been putting the world to rights."

"Michael you promised. Stop being so secretive."

I kept my attention focused on the road, but I knew I'd have to answer her curiosity. She waited.

"I can't tell you now. I'm not sure how I'm going to handle it, but I can tell you that it's going to be spectacular."

"Sounds ominous."

"It's definitely worth waiting for."

"You're starting to scare me."

"There's nothing to be scared of."

I kept one hand locked on the steering wheel and placed my other on her knee, trying to reassure her.

"Don't worry Becky, everything is under control."

"And you will tell me?"

"You won't be able to miss it."

"What do you mean?"

"All hell is going to break loose."

She squeezed my hand. I laughed and winked at her.

"Stick close when the fireworks start flying and you'll be fine."

We drove into the school and I was filled by an urge to pull onto the fields where I'd been humiliated during physical education by a teacher whose lustful enthusiasm for watching his charges grapple in the mud had always been disconcerting and spin the car in a series of reckless handbrake turns with the stereo turned up. I regained control and lazily stuck to the footpaths that led to the parking area. The school was a fraction of the size I remembered it being. It wasn't the inescapable fortress that had contained and constrained the youth who had tripped from detention to suspension and narrowly avoided expulsion. There were no walls, no barbed wire and no machine gun turrets; it was a summer camp, like taking a lazy stroll through the daisies. Its evil had been exorcised and only the lonely corridors and fabricated classrooms remained. I parked at an angle, boxing a Mercedes and a Porsche in and cast my eyes around a motley assortment of vehicles, the choices of a weak coalition. Public education was the glue that held the class divide together and working class transport sat uncomfortably alongside upper class superiority. For one evening only they'd have to trust one another, regardless of politics or income.

Turning the engine off, I walked around the car and opened the passenger door, convinced that Becky's father was tracking me, chewing dirt and examining my tracks, a feather in his cap and a musket strapped to his back. The party had already begun and an early dance engulfed the gymnasium that had been given over to the role of housing the function. Sitting at the doorway, behind an old school desk, was a plump mousy woman, who on sighting us switched on her cheery infection and greeted us with a fake vigour that a blind drunkard would have seen for what it really was – forced and tedious.

"Hi, welcome to the reunion. Can I see your invitations?"

I tried to put a name to her face. She'd put on a little weight, around forty pounds, but there was no mistaking that nihilistic charm. Claire Donovan. I remembered Blake telling me, after she'd given him a blowjob in his mother's car that she could suck a golf ball through a hosepipe and I wondered if she still had that same youthful lung capacity. We handed our cards over; she glanced at them casually and wrote on some paper with a marker pen. One of the school issue ones that I'd tried get high from by removing the top and inhaling the fumes. She looked up, sham smile in place and handed us each a square of the stationary that she'd been scrawling on. A Post-it note with 'Michael Flanagan' scribbled on in big, bold childlike letters.

"And, why exactly do I need this?" I asked, and noticing a similar badge stuck to her sagging left breast added, "Claire?"

She'd obviously explained her system at least one hundred times and tirelessly launched herself into the spiel.

"So that anyone who sees it will think 'Oh, it's Michael, I wonder what he's been up to?'."

I listened, nodded intently and feigned interest.

"And do you think that anyone is really interested in what I've been doing?" "Of course they are silly. It's not every day that you get to meet a rock star."

If they already knew, why did I have to wear the stupid fucking tag? I wanted to have the final word, to tell the smug bitch what she could do with her label. Something that involved a broom handle, lubricant and a pit bull terrier called Joe and I swear I was about to let fly when Becky grabbed my hand and dragged me through the door.

"What the hell has got into you?" she hissed.

"Nothing, I feel great."

"Then what was all that about?" she asked, jabbing a finger toward the obese queen of the 80s scene.

"I was having some fun that's all."

"Please don't embarrass me Michael," she implored.

I looked into her eyes and could easily have lost myself in them, swimming forever in their innocence and beauty.

"That's the last thing I want to do Becky."

"You promise?"

"I promise."

"Alright then. Let's get it over with. Get in there and mingle."

I adjusted to the dirge that the DU was churning out and found that if I ignored it, it became a dull hum. Pumping up the volume and stating that there's no limits is fine if you're twelve years old with a face full of acne, but to anyone over the age of twenty-five it's roughly the equivalent of listening to someone scrape their fingernails down a blackboard. The other parolees saw the celebrity and started to flock toward me, in dribs and drabs at first, then when they were certain that I wouldn't turn them away, the trickle became a tsunami. I smiled pleasantly and patiently answered all their questions. No, I didn't know Madonna, yes I was sure, I'd remember her if I had met her wouldn't I? No, I didn't know if anyone was planning to remake 'Logan's Run' and no, I didn't think that it would be a smashing idea to write a musical about the life of Martin Luther. Yes it was true that we picked our own support acts and if your brother's band wanted a shot, we'd have to hear a tape first. Yes, that's right, send it to the label, addressed to me and I'd listen to it as soon as I could. Out of the corner of my eye, I saw Taylor talking to the Evans twins who were enthralled by his every word. I strained to hear what he was saying and grinned as he told them how he had trained to be a vascular surgeon, but had opted for paediatrics, which was far more rewarding and how following his cases through to the end and knowing that his patients made a full recovery was the only reward he desired. I waved, indicating that I'd catch up with him later. He nodded and returned the wave. I turned to Becky and stared at her.

"Stop it Michael. Stop staring at me."

"Why?"

"Because it makes me uncomfortable. Makes me think that either my make up is running down my face or I've spilled something on my dress."

"Your face paint's fine and as far as I can tell whatever you've put in your mouth, you've swallowed."

"Don't be rude. Stop staring."

"I can't help it."

She glanced at her feet and murmured, "Please stop it Michael."

I shrugged, gave in and returned to the questions that I was being bombarded by. Elliot swaggered in and made a beeline straight for me, ignoring everyone who tried to stop him and chat. He really was a cocksure, arrogant little fucker. He brushed past Becky and interrupting another inane interrogation, began speaking.

"Hey Flanagan, why didn't you call me back?"

"I was busy."

"Yeah. Busy doing nothing, moping around, feeling sorry for yourself."

"Whatever. What did you want?"

"You were supposed to pick me up, remember? I had to catch a fucking taxi."

"Ah, poor baby. You have to phone them as well? Hurt your dialling finger did you?"

My confidence surprised him; he wasn't used to being put down. I thought he was going to flare up and prepared myself for Krakatoa Kurtz. He just stared at me.

"Where were you? I was waiting for you to call."

"I was out, okay? Do I need you to sign a permission slip whenever I want to do anything? Get off my fucking back. So I forgot to pick you up, sue me."

He shook his head, still staring at me.

"Take a fucking pill Flanagan, calm down. I only asked where you were. Chill."

He stood in front of Becky and didn't even know she was there and almost certainly didn't care either. I walked around him and stood by her side.

"You remember Becky, don't you Elliot?"

He ogled her, fixed on her breasts and crooned, "Doctor Becky, how you doing?"

"I'm fine Elliot. How are you?"

"Couldn't be better. Still supporting this dead beat. But, hey, what are friends for? If you can't rely on your friends, who can you rely on eh, Flanagan?"

"Whatever you say, Elliot."

"It was nice seeing you again Doc, but we've got things to do, haven't we Flanagan?"

"No."

"What?"

"I'm here with Becky. If there's somewhere you'd rather be, feel free. Don't let me stop you."

"Would you excuse us, Doc?" he said, pulling me to one side.

"Give me a minute would you?" I asked Becky, relenting and letting Elliot drag me away.

"You're here with her?"

"Yeah, I'm here with her."

"I didn't think she was your type."

"What's that supposed to mean?"

"Well, she's not a slut and as far as I know, hasn't had a starring role in any of your beloved movies."

"And that's what you think my type of woman is? Maybe you don't know me as well as you think you do."

"Do you know who I talked to today Flanagan? Alison. She's here and she wants to see you. Ditch Plain Jane and get with the plan."

Alison was here. She was here and she wanted to see me. After ten years she wanted to see me. I looked at Becky. Becky who had said yes, Becky, who believed in me and would stand by me no matter what. Through thick and thin, rich and richer. I stared at her and spoke to Elliot.

"Just let me go tell her, okay?"

"It's your fantasy not mine Flanagan."

I walked over to Becky and smiled. She smiled back, and Alison could have been a million miles away, she could have been anywhere. I didn't care.

"I've got to take care of something. I won't be long."

"What?"

"It doesn't matter. It's not important."

She hesitated before speaking.

"She's here, isn't she?"

"Who?"

"Who do you think Michael? Alison. She's here, you're going to see her and forget all about me."

I guess Elliot got a kick out of watching Becky break down. He was smiling, that sly, impertinent grin of his that always emerged when someone else was suffering.

119

"It's not what you think Becky."

"You suddenly know what I'm thinking do you Michael? Are you psychic?"

"No, that's not what I meant..."

"Then what did you mean?"

"I don't know."

"Let me make it easy for you okay? Go and see her, sort it out. If you come back, fine and if you don't...you don't."

"I'll be back, I swear."

"We'll see Michael, we'll see."

She smiled again and in her sad smile I heard Taylor's voice. I wanted to take her in my arms and hold her as the seasons changed. Hold her as spring became summer, the leaves fell from the trees and autumn gave way to the snow of winter. It had to end. Becky strolled over to where Taylor was still entertaining his audience and laughed as the heir apparent to the throne of bullshit explained exactly how he had come to win the Victoria Cross while serving in the Gulf War.

"Alright Elliot, I'm all yours."

He laughed. "That's the Flanagan I know."

I sighed. The Flanagan he'd known was dead and only Michael remained. Elliot led me to one of the far corners of the gym, the one where they used to keep the crash mats. The crash mats that I'd practised my stage diving technique on during my wasted school days, climbing to the top of the wall bars and hurling myself off with reckless abandon. Hoping to God that I'd land evenly and wouldn't shatter my spine or snap my neck.

Alison. The flesh I'd seen exposed, revealed but never tasted; the calorific embrace of departed youth. My folly, my torment stood chatting amiably to someone I didn't recognise. I searched for his name on the tag he displayed. Mark Davies. The name meant nothing to me. His disguise covered a body I was unfamiliar with. I tried to place him and nothing came to mind. I approached her slowly.

"Hello Alison."

She spun around, flicking her hair, an all over tan displaying the wealth she'd accumulated. Recognition flashed across her face and she offered me an incredibly well rehearsed smile.

"Flanagan, how are you?"

I stared at her. Watched the way her succulent lips said my name, the way her breasts heaved with every breath, the way her hair danced in the breeze.

I watched her and felt nothing.

"I prefer Michael, I'm fine. And you?"

She seemed slightly stunned by my response and in an attempt to take control of the conversation, resorted to cheap shock tactics.

"Busy as always. There's no end of people to fuck or cocks to suck and as long as the money's there, I'm happy to oblige."

"Lights, camera, action, go. Take the money and run huh?"

"Something like that, yeah," she laughed.

A West Coast drawl kept creeping into her voice, elongating her phrasing. "And what about you? Work keeping you busy?"

"Yeah, we're finishing the new record."

"Oh really?"

The least she could have done was to pretend to show a little interest. It wouldn't have been that difficult.

"Yeah, I'm sticking to the same old pattern, three chord trickery. Bang them out as fast as I can and hope it's good enough to keep the wolves at bay for another year."

"I've got a confession to make Flanagan. I don't actually own any of your records. I didn't know you'd made any until Elliot told me."

"They're not everybody's cup of tea."

"I will pick them up, I promise. I'm always working; I haven't really got time for a social life."

It's odd how one sentence can change your life. I thought about how much time I'd devoted to pursuing her career, thought that perhaps she still had a place in her heart for me. I thought that I was worth more than an apology and an afterthought.

"That's alright. You can't convert the world."

"Elliot's been telling me that you're a big fan of my work. You like what I do then Flanagan?"

"Yeah Flanagan, do you like what she does?" smirked Elliot.

I remembered each and every time he'd tried to humble me, hold me down and maintain the control he had over my life.

"It's...ah...it's different."

"It's alright to admit it. It doesn't make you a pervert. I like it, knowing that you're out there, watching me fuck. It's a real turn on."

"It turns you on, knowing that I've watched your films?"

"Watch your films," corrected Elliot.

"Oh yeah, it really turns me on. Thinking about you getting off on watching me being fucked by two or three guys," she purred.

She slipped her hand inside her trousers; the small, angular motion forced her knuckles against the zip, which bulged outward. She pulled her hand out, placed her index finger in her mouth and sucked it leisurely, seductively. Elliot watched her, stroked his lips and gazed at me, searching for a reaction.

"How does it make you feel Flanagan? Watching me like that. Does it turn you on?"

I didn't know what kind of sick game they were trying to play with me, but I knew that it was going to be the last time that I'd let Elliot fuck with my mind. So I played along to give him one last laugh.

"Yeah, it turns me on."

"I knew it would. I knew you'd feel what I feel, lying in front of the camera, waiting, ready to explode."

"What do you want me to say? I like watching you. What else do you want from me?"

"What do I want? I want you to fuck me."

"Right here? In front of everyone?"

"Whatever you want. We can do it here or we can go outside. It's entirely up to you."

"Okay. Let's go outside."

She smiled at Elliot, who winked at her as she took my hand and led me through the fire escape. Led me behind the gym where we used to smoke illicit cigarettes and she'd tell me how unfair her sex life was. She forced me back into the wall and knelt down. I felt her hand tug at my zip, felt her free my erection and felt her tongue licking its tip. Felt her take me in her mouth and thought about the time I'd longed for her to do it. Longed to tell her how she made me feel. Longed for her to tell me she loved me the way I loved her. I thought about Becky and knew that Alison wouldn't and couldn't love me the way I used to love her. I put my palm on her forehead and pushed her away. She fell backwards and landed on the concrete. She lay there, breathing heavily, staring at me, her eyes smouldering with anger and confusion.

"What's wrong? I thought this was what you wanted?"

She spat and propped herself up on her elbows. I couldn't move, couldn't speak. I could only think about Becky as Alison lay in front of me, her fury slowly rising to a crescendo.

"I thought you loved me," she hissed.

So did I. I thought that I'd loved her. I thought I'd wanted and needed her to satisfy a part of myself that I'd lost and could only see in the darkness, howling at the moon.

"This isn't love," I whispered.

"It isn't? Then what else would you call it Flanagan? If it isn't love, what is it?"

"It's what you do. It's the only thing you can do. It's all you are and all you ever will be."

"Am I that bad Flanagan? Is what I do so repugnant that you can't bear to touch me? Can't stand the thought of having to share me?"

I shook my head and reached down to help her to her feet. She brushed my arm away, glared at me and struggled to stand under her own power.

"No it isn't. It was your choice, not mine. It isn't what I want."

"And what do you want Flanagan?"

"I want my life back. I want all the things I've missed. I want to be Michael again and not some shadow who hides himself away."

"Elliot was right about you Flanagan," she laughed bitterly.

Elliot. He was the root of all my nightmares, the cancer that had spread my fear and the tumour that I had to cut out.

"He was huh? And what did Elliot say about me?"

"He said that you were a pathetic, lonely man, too scared to live and too frightened of dying to do anything."

"Maybe that's who I used to be, but it isn't who I am anymore."

"Flanagan?"

"Yeah?"

"Did you ever love me?"

Had I ever loved her? Ever felt the need to declare my undying devotion and shelter her from the maelstrom of cause and effect that had shaped our lives? Or was it familiarity that I'd clung to? A part of the past that prevented me acknowledging my cowardice? I gazed at her and thought of the pleasures that would never be mine. I wanted to remember her as she was here; confused, vicious and manipulative and not as the figure of lust who had been the main attraction in a thousand hollow performances I'd fixated by for far too long.

"I don't know. I think I might have, once. A long time ago. Goodbye Alison."

I turned and went back through the fire doors. 'Walking On Sunshine' by Katrina And The Waves was playing and the floor was filled with couples engaged in spastic jerks, hopelessly trying to recall the dance moves they'd learned from watching 'Top Of The Pops'. I walked over to the table that was doubling as a bar and signalled for a beer and received a can of Heineken. I popped the ring and tried to locate Becky. She stood on the outskirts of Taylor's increasing harem, her amusement growing as his lies increased. The more magnificent the untruth is, the more likely it is that people will lap it up. I decided to join her and was leaving the security of the bar, when I felt a hand tap me on the shoulder. I rotated my head and Elliot's grinning face greeted me.

"That was quick Flanagan. Did you enjoy yourself?" he giggled.

"Nothing happened."

"Yeah right. After all the build up and expectation, nothing happened. Shoot your bolt straight away did you? Or couldn't you get it up?"

"Nothing happened."

"You couldn't get it up could you? I know she was raring to go, so it has to be you. Don't worry Flanagan, I won't tell a soul. It'll be our little secret," he said, making a shushing noise, holding his finger to his lips.

"Haven't we got enough secrets without adding another to the menu? Nothing happened. I didn't want it to."

"Damn shame Flanagan. You don't know what you're missing."

"And you do?"

He shrugged.

"I couldn't let you partake without sampling the goods first, could I? It wouldn't have been fair."

"What?"

"What do you think I've been doing all day Flanagan? Sitting at home, twiddling my thumbs, waiting for you to call? I was with Alison. Making sure that she'd live up to your expectations and be everything you wanted."

"Let me get this straight Elliot. You fucked Alison today?"

"This afternoon to be exact."

"You knew how I felt and you went right ahead and did it anyway?"

"Hey, you don't have to thank me. I was just looking out for you."

"Looking out for me?"

"Sure, same way I always have. Had to let her know all about you, didn't I?"

"And the bit where you fucked her, how does that fit into the picture?"

"You know. You start talking, having a few drinks and before you know it, one thing leads to another. A little gratitude wouldn't go amiss here Flanagan."

"Gratitude? You arrogant bastard! I hope you enjoyed it Elliot, because while you were sticking it to Alison, you know what I was doing? I was firing you."

His grin disappeared.

"Firing me?"

"Firing you." I nodded. "Getting rid of your ugly arse, kicking you out, giving you the chop."

"You fired me?"

"Uh huh. Pick up the music papers tomorrow; they're covering it in detail. Front man gets his marching orders."

"You can't do that," he whispered.

"Too late fucko! I already did."

"It's my band. You can't do this to me. I made you what you are."

"And what's that Elliot? A pathetic, lonely man who's too scared to live? Well, guess what? I'm not frightened anymore."

"You can't do this. The label won't let you."

"No? You sure about that? Maybe they're just as sick of your worthless shit as I am. Maybe they were thrilled when I told them. Maybe they're partying right now, celebrating their good fortune. The pariah's finally gone and with him goes all of his tedious shit."

"Why Flanagan? Why fire me?"

"Why? Pick a fucking reason. There are a million of them, each one as valid as the next. I'm tired of playing second fiddle to your ego, tired of watching you piss everything away, tired of having to apologise to all the people who have to deal with your tantrums, and tired of you. I'm sick of you pushing me around, sick of you always getting what you want regardless of who it hurts. You want me to carry on? I've got all night."

"This isn't happening."

"Face it Elliot, it's happened."

"I'll change, give me a chance and I'll change. Everything will be different, just give me another chance," he babbled.

"I can't. It was either you or me and as soon as I realised that, I made the call." "You can't do this to me, I won't let you."

"You won't let me? Fuck you Elliot, it's over."

"No, fuck you Flanagan," he screamed as he leapt at me.

He must have hit me pretty hard, we both ended up on the floor, rolling around trying to hit each other. But as he once pointed out, I'm bigger than he is. I used my weight to pin him down, and started to pound him, hitting him over and over again. I remember humming that song from 'The Wizard of Oz', the one that appears just after Judy Garland drops out of the sky and her house squashes that green bitch flat; the one about the wicked old witch being good and dead. At the end of every verse I yelled at him.

"How does it feel motherfucker? How does it feel?"

The guests lost any interest they'd previously had in strutting to their teen anthems and the polished wooden floor cleared faster than lies flow from a politician's mouth. A fight will do that and even though it was totally one sided; cheers still rang through the gym. Everyone was there to remember their school days and there I was, helping them to relive them. Okay, so I didn't take his lunch money or give him a Chinese burn, but I beat him to within a few metres of his life. Taylor eventually came to his rescue. He'd taken his time because I think he wanted me to do it, that he wanted it to last as long as possible and that he found it quite gratifying to see me slap the holy hell out of Elliot. But nothing lasts forever and reluctantly he eventually stepped in and wrestled me from my quarry.

"He's had enough Michael. He's had enough."

I stared blankly at Taylor and looked down at Elliot. He was crying and had drawn himself into a ball, clutching his knees to his chest.

"See you around Kuntz," I muttered

I gazed at the faces that had formed a circle around Elliot and myself, saw their bloodlust, heard them whispering and felt Taylor tugging at my arm.

"Are you alright Michael?" he asked. "Yeah, I'm done," I replied flatly.

I pushed my way through the spectators and strolled briskly to the entrance, flipping the bird at Claire as she huffed and puffed and tried to escape the desk that her bulk was trapped behind. Laughing maniacally, I jumped in my car and twisted the key in the ignition, rammed the accelerator down and peeled out of the school, the tires screeching in protest. I drove, how long for I don't know, through the streets that formed the grid pattern of the town. I ended up back at the dead common that had been teeming with life ten hours previously. I parked, left the car open and walked to the edge of the cliffs and sat there gazing at the waves as they crashed against the rocks. I didn't hear Becky approach and only became aware that she was there when I heard her voice.

"Michael, is that you?"

"Yeah."

She came over, sat down and put an arm around my shoulder. "Are you alright?"

"Yeah."

"What happened back there?"

"I fired Elliot."

"You fired him?"

"Uh huh."

"Why?"

"Because he's a prick."

"I could have told you that Michael. What I meant was, why wait until now?"

"I don't know it's hard to explain. I always knew what Elliot was like, but I never realised it until I came back here. I never realised the effect he'd had on me. I took a long look at myself and I didn't like what was staring back at me. I had to try and do something about it."

"And that meant firing Elliot?"

"Maybe. Elliot was just a part of it."

She laughed.

"I don't understand you Michael."

"I'm a complicated guy Becky."

"I'm beginning to see that. Can I ask you a question?"

"Ask away."

"When you left, back at the reunion, did you go to see Alison?"

I smiled.

"Yes, I did."

"What happened?"

"Nothing."

"Nothing? Are you sure...I mean..."

"Nothing happened. We talked."

"That was all you did? Talk?"

"Yeah."

"What did you talk about?"

"Not a lot. She told me that she wanted to fuck me because I was her biggest fan and the most pathetic individual that she had ever met. Said it turned her on knowing that a loser was obsessed with her."

"And did you?"

"Did I what?"

"Did you fuck her?"

I sighed.

"No I didn't, I think she couldn't believe that anyone would turn her down and it brought her back down to Earth with a bang. Why do you want to know?"

"I don't...It's that...You were there with me and I..."

"You didn't want to think that I was still in love with her and that as soon as she showed up I'd go running after her like I always used to. It's okay, I talked to Taylor earlier."

"You did? What did he tell you?"

"He told me that you were in love with me. That you've always been in love with me. He said that I should open my eyes, see what I've got instead of looking for a reason not to."

She stared at the waves as they smashed into the cliffs.

"He told you that?"

"Yeah. So, is it true?"

"Is what true Michael?"

"What Taylor said? Do you love me?"

"Yes Michael, it's true. It's always been true."

"Why didn't you tell me?"

"I did. I told you last night."

"No, I mean why didn't you tell me before?"

"Would it have made any difference?"

"No, I don't suppose it would. I don't know, I can't say. It all seems so sudden."

"Not for me it isn't. I've been living with it for fifteen years."

"And now?"

"Nothing's changed. I still feel the same."

"Fifteen fucking years and you didn't say a thing. Fucks with your head doesn't it?"

"No."

"If you say so. You're the doctor."

"So, where do we go from here?"

"Well, I fly back to Boston on Sunday. I've got a record to finish."

"Oh."

"Why don't you come with me? I've got a spare ticket now that Elliot is history."

"Just like that? Drop everything and fly half way around the world with you?"

"Why not?"

"Because this is where I belong Michael. I've got responsibilities; I can't just go off with you."

"Becky, a friend gave me some advice today. He said that life was taking risks. If you don't grab your chances when they appear you'll spend the rest of your days regretting that you didn't."

"Taylor said that to you?"

"He did."

"And you believed him?"

"Yup. And he was right. I guess there's a first time for everything."

"Why don't you stay Michael?"

"I can't. I've got to go back and I'm asking you to go with me."

"I know you are."

"Well?"

"Well what?"

"Jesus fucking H. Christ! Are you going to come with me?"

"I don't know."

"I've already wasted ten years of my life Becky. I don't want to waste another ten dwelling on the fact that I let you slip away."

"Michael?"

"Yeah?"

"What's it like in Boston?"

"It's beautiful. Like you."

"Oh, for fuck's sake. Alright I'll go with you."

"You will?"

"I've already said I will haven't I? Do you need a picture?"

"No, but it might help."

"Michael?"

"Uh huh?"

"Shut up."

"Yes Doctor Connolly. Becky?"

'Yes Michael?"

"I'm sorry I ruined the party."

"I know."

"No, I mean it. I'm sorry I embarrassed you."

"I know you are."

"Do you forgive me?"

"Yes Michael, I forgive you."

"Thank you."

"Michael?"

"Yes Becky?"

"Will you please shut up?"

As we sat on the cliffs watching the waves roll in, I thought about the old man who used to search through the ocean's debris and tell stories to a young boy. I thought about him and laughed as the birds circled endlessly above the sea.

Epilogue – February 22nd, 1999

The new record didn't exactly set the charts on fire. It didn't flop, but it wasn't the raging success that I'd thought it would be. Bill told me it was because we fucked with fate and sprung the whole thing on Joe Public with no warning. He says the next album will slay them and break all sales records for a punk band.

He says a lot of things that I don't believe. Sometimes when we're on stage and I'm standing behind a microphone that's smashed me in the teeth for the twentieth time that night I think I maybe made the wrong decision when I fired Elliot. But then I look around and see Charlie giving one hundred and ten percent, flying into the pit and playing like there's no tomorrow and I know I was right. The last thing I heard about Elliot was that he was trying to put a new band together, living off the fact that he used to be famous and that he's been seeing a lot of Alison. Good luck to them, they deserve each other.

Taylor was right. Blake did re-offend. By the time they caught up with him, he'd raped and murdered three women. One of them had been married and had a daughter called Jane who was eleven years old. They showed her funeral on the evening news. There was a good turn out and a lot of people cried. Blake was attacked while he was being held on remand. His eyes were gouged out and his tongue was removed. They never found his tongue. Taylor said that one of the cons probably kept it as a trophy. I can relate to that.

Taylor's having a grand old time. He's still seeing the Evans twins and told me a story about the night of the reunion that made my stomach turn. I'm not sure that you can actually do what he described or that it's even legal. He quit his job. Told his boss to go fuck himself, and now he's the head of security for the band. He bounces over anxious kids off the stage and slaps anyone he doesn't like the look of. The label's happy that I've got the big, flabby motherfucker as a bodyguard and Taylor's happy because he's getting to do all the things he dreamt of as a child. Hitting people and seeing the world.

Becky moved in as soon as we landed and she's still here. She joined a private practice and the patients love her. I think it's her accent. The money's great and she's kept busy. The subject of kids crops up now and then, a few bambinos to carry the Flanagan line into immortality, but I'd rather wait and see how everything plays out. She still has nightmares and I watch her as she twists and turns, moaning softly. I watch her and try to remember what it was like to have my dreams invaded. It scares me sometimes, but she knows I'm there if she needs to talk. She knows that I'll listen and understand.

Me? I'm adjusting. Slowly. It was weird being the centre of attention and I've tried to make sure that all the promotional duties are shared equally by the band. Show that we're not a one trick pony. Charlie grumbles about having nothing to say and when he does, I tell him to make it up. He does and the press love him. I don't dream anymore. If I do, I don't remember them. Maybe the ghosts have finally packed their bags and left. Maybe they're just waiting; waiting for me to relax. If they are, they're going to be waiting a long time. Welcome to my life. Welcome to my show.

If you enjoyed Compression, here is a chapter from Tim's new book, 'What Would Gary Gygax do?', which will be published soon.

A Paladin, an Elf and a Ranger walk into a tavern…

"The room is pitch black. You can't see anything, but you can hear a clicking and shuffling…"

"I've got a torch, I'm going to light it. What can I see?"

"And while he's doing that I'm getting ready to cast a magic missile at whatever it is that's making that noise."

"The room seems to explode in light as your torch comes to life, and after quickly adjusting to the sudden illumination, you see a skeleton, dressed in rusting chain mail, sword in one hand, shield in the other. He charges toward you…"

And that's how my first game of Dungeons & Dragons started way back in 1983. Okay, so it didn't actually start like that; the obligatory meeting in a tavern, being hired by a rich merchant to find a fabulous jewel that he needed in order to pay for his daughter's dowry (or so he told us gullible adventurers) and the descent into the dark depths of the dungeon in which said item was located, all preceded that encounter. But it was my first taste of action in a game. The jolt of excitement that coursed through me, sending nervous shivers down my spine as I made my first combat roll was incredible, it was almost as though my ten year old self had suddenly stumbled across the purpose and meaning of life in that one random die roll that determined my fate on that cold, crisp Sunday afternoon. In that moment of imaginary planetary alignment and stellar conjunction, it all made sense to me and I knew that nothing would ever be the same again. I'd had my first taste of gaming and thus began my lifelong, sometimes secret, sometimes not, obsession.

It's hard to explain the appeal of, and what's so intriguing and exciting about, D&D and RPGs unless the person you're explaining it to knows what you're talking about or has actually played. In which case, you're already preaching to the armoured, hack 'n' slash choir as they know exactly what you're talking about. Trying to explain it someone who knows nothing about it though, that's something else entirely, as it doesn't matter what you say, it always sounds…well, sort of geeky. Which is fine and dandy, if like me, you're already a geek and proud to be so. Not so much for most people though, as every single time I've attempted to explain the all-encompassing magnificence of the game to them, they have usually replied in one of three ways. Sighed, given me that 'there, there' look, rolled their eyes and muttered something along the lines of 'Nerd', or, more commonly, they burst into uncontrollable fits of giggles, and when they've managed to catch their breath, have stared at me and just said "Really?" That answer, look and laugh when combined, for some reason unknown to the human psyche, makes any comeback, or thought of countering with a pithy anecdote almost impossible. And lastly, there's the response that I haven't encountered for nearly thirty years, which mainly involved getting punched in the side of the head and being told to "Fuck off!". That was my favourite. Oh yes, I used to love that one best of all.

After constantly repeating the same futile exercise, you'd think I'd just give in, wave the white flag and admit defeat. If Einstein immediately recognised the insanity of repetition and expecting a different outcome, you'd think that after three decades that maybe, just maybe, I'd get it too. And if it was anything other than D&D, I probably would. However, the older that you get, the more you realise that there are very few constants in life, and that, more often than not, even friends don't number among them. Dungeons and Dragons, punk rock and comics though, they've always been there for me, and I for them. Relationships, trends, jobs and all of that boring nine to five rigmarole, it comes and goes, but D&D is as constant as the North Wind and the anger of Crom.

See, I could witter on about the connections to mythology, history and legend, the links to literature and film, the creativity of imagination and how problem solving aids lateral thinking. I could talk about its escapist value and the need to find a way to relieve the increasingly confining and debilitating repression forced on all of us by a system we're imprisoned by and perpetuate through the enslavement of work. I could do that, but I won't. Because, it's all of those things and so much more, but at the end of the day, when you really get down to the nitty gritty and disassemble Dungeons and Dragons, it's a social thing. Like poker night. Except you don't lose any money, which means that you don't upset your partner, which means (theoretically) that you still get laid. And you get to slay monsters, explore far off distant lands, encounter all manner of strange and marvellous creatures and places and bizarre people. You get to kill, maim and destroy without fear of recrimination or revenge and without worrying about doing serious gaol time for any misdemeanours or social faux paus you may or may not commit within the game. It's like playing a video game, but you get to hang out with your friends and avoid becoming a pasty loner afraid of the sun and everything beyond the confines of your bedroom door. You'll still be pasty and you'll still be terrified of the daunting power of Sol and all of the nasty, hidden dangers of the outside world, but at least you'll have friends. Dungeons and Dragons. It gets you laid, helps you make friends and it's cheaper and far less tiresome and boring than therapy. Go on, admit it. You want to play, don't you? Then pull up a chair, grab a D20 and let's begin.

Oh, and that skeleton? I smashed its skull in twain and made a necklace out of its teeth. That's how I roll…

If you would like to pre-order Tim's new book, send an e-mail to louise@earthisland.co.uk